WICKED CITY

A Sam Raven Thriller

Brian Drake

WOLFPACK
PUBLISHING
— EST 2013 —

WOLFPACK
PUBLISHING
— EST 2013 —

Wicked City
Paperback Edition
Copyright © 2021 Brian Drake

Wolfpack Publishing
5130 S. Fort Apache Road 215-380
Las Vegas, NV 89148

Paperback ISBN 978-1-64734-563-1
Ebook ISBN 978-1-64734-557-0

WICKED CITY

WICKED CITY

PROLOGUE

It was a hot night.

Sam Raven waited in a cluster of trees near the Athens University of Economics & Business. The trees shielded him from the street. The daytime heat of Athens extended to the three a.m. hour, the temperature on his cell showing 78 degrees. He couldn't help but sweat under his jacket and shoulder holster.

All was quiet but for the occasional taxi or car. The bus service had ceased hours ago. To Raven's right, a fence closed off a circular track connected to a gym.

Careful planning had brought Raven to this moment. He needed to collect an informant who knew a group of jihadists had a weapon of mass destruction. Usually, he took a more direct approach—turning over informants to the CIA wasn't his style. *Shooting* terrorists was his style. But the informant, a woman, didn't want to see her father, the lead jihadist, killed in a gun battle.

Raven's status of ex-operative with friends in both high and low places was the reason she'd sought him out.

He'd been in Athens for R&R when the tan-skinned beauty with long black hair and seductive eyes found him at a beach side bar. She wore the thin wrap around her shoulders concealing the toned body in the blue bikini.

She'd struck up a normal conversation and introduced herself as Shema. Another tourist alone in Athens. They met again the next day, and, at dinner, she brought up the real reason for meeting him.

"I need help, Sam."

"I was waiting for this part," Raven said, but not without a smile.

The five-star restaurant had made him get out a white tuxedo and red bow tie.

Shema Rafki wore a sparkling blue gown, which flowed over her slender body all the way to the ankles. Her dark hair kissed her smooth shoulders on the way down her back. If anybody had been able to see her heels, they'd have noticed the diamond studs on the cross straps.

They sat in a quiet booth with a flickering candle on the table providing the only light.

She frowned at his response. "You knew?"

"I figured," he said. "It's embarrassing how people find me sometimes. You'd think I'd make it harder in case they were trying to kill me."

"Not your style."

"No?"

"You know people need help. You know they need to find you, so you don't hide."

Raven sipped his martini. "What's the problem, Shema?"

"My father is Tarik Rafki."

"Should I know him?"

"Your face would have lost its color if you did," she said. "He's the number two man in the Abul Hosef Organization."

Raven put down his martini. "Now *his* name I recognize."

After al-Qaeda and ISIS came Abul Hosef, a radical Muslim intent on carrying on jihad across the globe. The bulk of his organization's activity had happened over the last six months. Bombings in Germany, London, and Rome. A mass shooting in Madrid. Hundreds dead. Thousands injured.

"Tell me more," Raven said.

"My father is here in Athens, collecting a bomb. He says it's a *dirty* bomb."

Raven maintained his poker face, but a chill ran up his neck. A combination of conventional explosives mixed with radioactive material. Such bombs kept the best and brightest in Western intelligence awake at night. The west had been fortunate no such weapon had ever been used, but there was a first time for everything.

Nobody ever expected terrorists to crash planes into buildings, either.

"Are you part of Abul Hosef?" he asked her.

She nodded. "I've known for a long time what my father is doing, but meetings, training in the desert, that's one thing. But buying a bomb—"

"Shema. Look me in the eye and repeat what you said."

She hesitated, dropped her eyes to the table.

"The Abul Hosef Organization has done more than have meetings and train in the desert, my dear," Raven said. "You're downplaying things a little."

"It *needs* to stop," she said. "It's *wrong*." She looked up at him. "I want out."

"Uh-huh."

"You can reach the Greek secret service or the Americans, right?"

"I know the Americans here, yeah."

"We're going to be here for two more weeks," she said. "I will provide you with information, and when my father takes delivery of the bomb, I will tell you where it is."

"And I call in the cavalry."

"I don't want you to kill him."

"I don't doubt you think your father can be redeemed—"

"You're insulting."

"I don't mean to be, Shema. Cases like this aren't usually as simple as *arresting* somebody."

She sat straight, put her chin out boldly. Her eyes didn't leave his.

"If he has to die, he has to die."

"Okay. How do you want to work this out?"

She explained her plan.

For two weeks Shema and Raven met. She filled him in on not only the cell's activity, but the rest of the organization, as she knew it. Raven planned to turn the notes over to the CIA. Their meetings were short, but both found time to give in to the attraction between them. When they said goodbye each time, Raven wondered if she'd live long enough to finish the task.

And now, two weeks later, the big night. Shema phoned and said she'd meet him at three a.m. at the bus stop near the economics school. Raven watched the bus stop from the trees. Together they could go to the Americans. Raven had phoned his local contacts, pals from his CIA days, and arranged the drop-off.

He checked his watch. 3:22. Shema was late.

He scanned his area again, only crickets keeping him company. Under his leather jacket, his Nighthawk Custom Talon .45 auto hung under his left arm. A pouch under his right arm secured two spare 10-round extended magazines. His rented Ford Mustang GT waited on the curb.

He was all set, but no Shema.

Tires screeched; an engine surged. Raven's pulse jumped. Incoming!

He jerked his head left, watching bright headlights flash around a corner. The black car skidded as it made the turn. The engine surged and the headlamps brightened Raven's hiding spot. The car veered off the road. The front end bumped the curb, the car speeding into the trees to smash into a thick trunk and come to a crushing stop.

The front of the car, now a crumpled V shape, only hinted at the damage beyond, which looked considerable. The driver's door swung open, and Shema Rafki fell half out of the car.

She put out her left hand to block her fall, but as Raven rushed to her, he knew the support she needed wouldn't be there. The fingers on her hand had been chopped off, leaving only bloody stumps.

Her face was no better, her nose and eyes and lips bleeding, swelling all around.

"Shema!"

She hit the ground, her upper body twisting with her legs still in the car. Raven pulled her out and lay her on the ground.

She breathed hard, arching her back in pain, coughing. Specks of blood landed on Raven's face.

"Shema?"

There were bloody patches staining her clothes up and down her body. Whatever had gone wrong, she had been discovered; Shema's father had been cruel indeed.

She choked out the words. "He *discovered*...said I betrayed...traitors...die—"

"Stay with me, Shema."

She said, "*Puh...puh...*"

"What?"

She summoned her strength and said, "*Purse.*" And her body went limp, her breath slowing. He started to move his right arm from behind her, but her eyes on his made him stop. She tried to smile and raised her other hand, the one with all the fingers intact, and touched his face. She let out a choked sob.

Raven took his arm from under her head and set her down gently and found the purse on the passenger seat. Phone, odds and ends, and a folded sheet of paper. He looked at the paper and used the flash from his cell phone to read the address.

He jammed the paper in a pocket. He knelt beside Shema once again, but it was already too late. She'd stopped breathing.

Raven stood and stepped away. His pulse thumped in his head.

This wasn't supposed to happen.

She hadn't wanted it like this. She'd tried to do the right thing, and bring her father to justice without violence, but now Raven had to finish the job.

Another engine surged. Headlamps shined on Raven and Shema's car as the second vehicle screeched to a stop short of the curb. The front doors flew open, two men jumping out. The passenger raised an automatic weapon.

Raven pivoted to face them, his right hand snaking under his jacket to grab the .45. He aimed the pistol in a two-hand grip and his index finger pressed the tuned trigger. The autoloader flashed flame and kicked four times. The passenger cried out as the hollow points split open the front of his chest and exploded out the back. His body crashed against the car before ever getting his weapon into action.

The driver stayed on his side and dropped to his knees, using the hood to shoot over. Raven put the Talon's glowing night sights on the driver's forehead.

The Talon barked again. The gunman's head snapped back, emptying a portion of its contents before his body tipped over to join the spill.

Raven lowered his gun, scanning left and right for further threats. None present. He slapped a 10-round magazine into the Talon and holstered the gun.

He might have failed to protect Shema, as he had failed to

protect so many before her, but now he'd show her father, Tarik Rafki, the meaning of payback.

He grabbed the dead passenger's weapon, a Heckler & Koch MP7 submachine gun. An extra magazine on the gunner's belt found a snug home in the inside pocket of Raven's jacket.

The V8 Mustang GT rumbled and carried him through the streets. Raven blew through lights to reach the address noted by Shema. He had no idea how her father had missed the clue. Maybe they hadn't bothered to look. Perhaps her old man only wanted her dead as an example to anybody else thinking of getting out. *If I'm willing to kill my own child, how harsh will your punishment be?*

Same old story. The villains of the world never changed.

Until Sam Raven came along. And they usually only changed to room temperature.

Raven drove by the address and gave it a passing glance. An empty two-level office building at the corner of an intersection. Signs out front advertised its availability for lease. Windows boarded. Raven parked the Mustang and returned on foot. He lowered the jacket zipper to allow access to his pistol.

He stopped at the corner across the street and examined the gray building. The boards around the windows held most of his attention. Lines of light from inside spilled out around the edges. A sliding door leading to an adjoining garage caught his attention. Glancing up at the edge of the roof, he watched a moment for patrols. If there were any there, they weren't looking over the edge.

He took out his cell and speed-dialed a number.

"You coming in, Sam?" said Harry Abel, the local CIA man.

"Plans changed. Shema's dead. I'm at a building on the corner of—" and he gave the location, adding: "You better get here before I level the place."

"Sam, wait. Sam!"

Raven ended the call and stowed the cell. He crossed the street at a trot clutching the MP7 close to his chest. He reached the wall near the sliding door and felt for a padlock. Easy enough. He fired a burst from the MP7. The noise would attract attention, sure, but the salvo did its job. The pieces of the padlock clattered onto the sidewalk.

Yelling inside reached Raven's ears as he lifted the sliding door. He slipped under and let the door drop shut behind him. Concrete floor, low light showing various pieces of litter strewn around. Half constructed walls and stray building equipment. He ran to the left, for a concrete pillar, as three gunners converged on his right across the open floor.

Two of the onrushing shooters stopped and shouldered their MP7s. Raven ducked around the pillar as they fired. He slid down the length of the smooth concrete to roll onto his belly. Holding the MP7 on its side because of the extended magazine, he triggered another burst. The shooters scattered. Raven fired again, the weapon clicking empty. Ricochets careened off concrete and bounced throughout the space.

Raven reloaded the MP7 as somebody shouted commands. Tarik Rafki, the boss. Where was he? A partial office sat ahead of Raven, the wood frame in place. Sheet rock only covered the frame on either side of the doorway. A stack of unused sheet rock jammed among the rest of the equipment in the space would make fine cover. Raven left the pillar and vaulted over the stack.

He stayed on his belly, peering around one side of the sheet rock stack, then sliding to the center. The shooters' footsteps smacked the floor as they converged. Raven took potshots through the gaps in the wooden frame. The shooters split, two heading for the alleged protection of the sheet rock near the doorway, the other for the pillar Raven had vacated.

Raven swung the MP7 to the doorway as the gunners cleared the space to open fire side-by-side. His first burst unzipped one gunner's neck. As he fell, he knocked his partner off balance, the second shooter firing over Raven's head. The shooter sought refuge behind the partial wall. Raven stitched his next burst through the wall, rewarded with a sharp scream and a thud.

The MP7 clicked empty again. Raven let it fall and drew his .45.

Feet shuffled behind him. The third gunner rushed from the pillar, but he only made two steps forward before the .45 pistol cut him down. Keeping his head low, Raven fired twice over the top of the stack he hid behind. The .45 slugs cut through the gunner's stomach and pelvis. He toppled forward, his body sliding with momentum into the stack of sheetrock.

Three down.

One left.

"Come out, Tarik!" Raven shouted. He stayed behind cover, raising his head enough to peer through the wooden frame.

"Mr. Raven, I presume?"

"Correct."

"It will be my pleasure to kill you, Mr. Raven!"

Raven rolled across the floor, stopping on his belly. He looked through the crisscrossing 2x4s of the wood frame for a target.

Tarik Rafki squatted by a wooden plank propped up as a table on a pair of saw horses. On the plank sat what Raven figured was his pet bomb, contained in a long black case. Behind him was a forklift, presumably used to carry the bomb from a truck to the table. Rafki wore a black suit, his head bald except for a strip of hair above his ears circling around the back of his head. He fired at Raven. The wooden frame splintered, Raven rolling right. He covered his face from the flying shards.

The forklift rumbled to life.

Raven rose to a knee and fired. Rafki reversed from the table and worked the forklift around to aim the blades in Raven's direction.

Raven moved fast. He jammed the .45 into his shoulder holster as he ran for one of the dead shooters' HKs, snatching up the MP7. The blades of the forklift crashed through the wood frame, 2x4s snapping and clattering, and plowed through the sheet rock. The wall pieces crumbling and filling the air with choking white dust. As the debris rained down, Raven ran. The forklift blades brushed his back as he moved, and he steered for another support pillar.

Gunfire burst from behind. The bullets whined off the pillar, sparking as they ricocheted. Chips of cement pelted Raven's face as he sought refuge once again.

Wood and sheet rock crunched as Tarik Rafki reversed the forklift, the hydraulic motor whining. The lifting chain brought the blades to a higher level. The motor rumbled again. Raven swung the MP7 around the side and let a burst go. Tarik Rafki bore down on Raven with the forklift blades high enough so the carriage support plate above the blades acted as a shield, blocking most of his body. Only a small bit of his face showed through the gap between the carriage and blades. He used his left hand to stick the MP7 out of the cabin and fire blindly.

The rounds missed but the forklift rolled closer. Raven had nowhere but open space around him, no other construction zones. He dropped the MP7 and grabbed for the Nighthawk Custom. With his two-hand grip, he rested the pistol on the side of the pillar and lined up the glowing sights.

Raven and Rafki fired at the same time, Raven setting his sights for a second shot. He had no idea where the jihadist's salvo went, but his bullet struck where he'd intended. Straight through the gap and into Rafki's right eye. In place of the white outer layer and dark center, there was only a bloody black hole fringed with torn flesh.

Tarik Rafki slumped forward, his dead weight keeping the accelerator down. Raven stepped aside as the forklift crashed into the cement pillar. It came to an abrupt stop with the motor still running.

Raven put his .45 away and ran for the sliding door. There was no sense gloating over the body. Shema was dead. Now the cavalry could secure the bomb and the Abul Hosef Organization would hurt a little. The CIA would act on any intelligence they found, and what Shema had provided in her meetings with Raven. He was confident the terror organization's days were numbered.

It was some consolation, but not what Raven would have preferred. He'd have *preferred* to take down the terrorists while keeping Shema alive.

By the time he reached the Mustang, two helicopters closed in on the building. Their spotlights shined on the empty street. Raven ignored them as they touched down in the intersection. Two groups of Greek special operators clad in black, with automatic weapons, jumped out. Raven started the car and drove away.

After traveling two blocks, he still hadn't caught his breath. His phone rang. He answered.

"Bomb's in a black case," Raven said.

"Found and secured," Harry Abel, the CIA man, said. "Where are you?"

"Already gone."

"Which one's Rafki?"

"Forklift."

"Okay. You all right?"

Raven hesitated while breathing hard. He said, "I'll be fine."

"The CIA thanks you for your service, Sam. Ever consider rejoining us?"

He clutched the cell phone tight in his left hand.

"It's better I stay alone," he said. He ended the call before Abel responded.

He felt something wet on his left cheek. Raven turned the rearview mirror to look. A smear of blood. Had he been hit? He touched his face and looked at the red on his fingertips. No. He knew where the blood had come from.

Shema's final touch.

CHAPTER ONE

It wasn't the kind of bar where one expected trouble, but Sam Raven arrived prepared. He wore his pistol under a gray sport coat out of habit born from a survival instinct he never switched off.

The upscale establishment in downtown Paris, a bar off the tourist trail, was packed. Plenty of coverage for a clandestine meeting; he and his contact wouldn't have to speak in hushed tones. The unintended consequence of such a crowd meant an enemy could hide easily. Raven had no intention of being there long, and knew the fastest way out was the back door to an alley.

He saw his contact at the bar with his shoulders hunched. Waiting as he said he would.

The hostess at the door, a short blonde woman with the top button of her blouse open so her pushed-up cleavage could play peek-a-boo, greeted him. Her exposed skin glistened with sweat. She said all tables were taken but one might open in fifteen to thirty minutes. Her eyes wandered up and down his tall frame, noting the expensive cut of his clothes.

Raven didn't mind the examination and might have done likewise under different circumstances. But not tonight. He didn't break eye contact with her. He smiled instead. "I have a friend waiting."

She made a sweeping gesture with her right hand. "Enjoy your evening."

He crossed the polished tile floor, almost noting his reflection. Polished any further than it was, he might be able to use the floor to shave.

The upper part of the far wall to his right was all mirror and reflected the portion of the bar to his left. The reflection gave the illusion of a much larger space.

He moved through the narrow space between tables, focused on his destination. His danger scan took in details around him at the same time.

Soft piano music filled the air, and the after-work crowd, still in their business attire, filled the room with conversation and light laughter. He didn't miss those details, either. Clusters of office associates celebrating a deal; couples trying to be discreet as they were more than likely married to other people; men on their way to one too many laying on a thick pick-up to attractive co-workers.

Same as many other bars, but the income levels at this place dwarfed their downtown counterparts. Raven heard only the native language. No tourists to muddy the place with smart-phone translators at full volume.

Raven noted all such details as he made a note of his return path to the front door and glanced ahead at the rear exit. His survival depended on knowing such information, but part of him wished he could relax with friends too. His life had taken a different path, and he'd long made his peace about where fate had directed his steps.

His informant, Dimitri, the only man alone in the crowd, sat with a comfortable hunch to his shoulders. He rested both arms on the bar and nursed a glass of beer. Raven shook his head. Dimitri, of all people, should have selected a table near a wall. He turned his head as Raven reached him and sat up. He indicated the empty stool beside him.

"I've been saving you the seat."

"Anybody try to fight you for it?"

Dimitri laughed. "They're polite here."

Raven sat. It took a moment to get the busy bartender's attention, but when he did, he said, "Martini. One shot of vodka Russian Standard, one shot of Tanqueray, and two olives." He didn't have to raise his voice.

The bartender nodded and started building the drink.

"Maybe we should have picked another place."

Dimitri laughed. "You have to line up at the door at two in the morning to get a table. But I like the crowd. Makes me feel less like a rat hiding in a corner."

Raven examined Dimitri. He had started in Moscow, but in recent years managed to find a home within a French drug syndicate. Raven had saved the man's life during his Moscow exit. Ever since, Dimitri had returned the favor by passing information of interest.

"You're putting on weight, Dimitri."

"Nuts, I thought I had dropped ten pounds."

"Other way around, actually."

Dimitri's black silk shirt stretched tight over his belly, which stuck out over his leather belt. Dark-skinned with a mop of black hair, Dimitri faced Raven with sleepy eyes.

"Stress," the informant said.

"It will ruin the best of us. Keeping busy?"

"Non-stop," Dimitri said.

"I bet."

Recent high-profile arrests as France tried to control the nation's drug problem had kept Dimitri from his beauty sleep and around junk food.

Raven's martini arrived. The bartender placed the chilled glass on a blue napkin monogrammed with the bar's name. Raven thanked the man, swallowed a sip, and ate one olive.

Dimitri examined Raven's face. "You look a little rough yourself."

"I was in Athens last two weeks," Raven said. He swallowed some of his martini, his eyes distant.

"Was it bad?" Dimitri said.

Raven set down the glass. "Yes, it was bad."

"I understand."

A beat of silence passed between the two men, but the bar remained jubilant.

"Your dinner tonight?" Dimitri pointed at the two olives, his belly convulsing with a forced laugh.

Raven appreciated the change in tone. "Two olives a day keeps you in fighting shape. You should consider the diet."

"Uh-huh." Dimitri drank some beer.

"Tell me what's going on," Raven said, "and how much will it cost?"

"I need to get out."

"Again?"

"Again."

"Got a stake?"

"I need a little more."

"How much?"

"I'll let you decide the worth. There is trouble in the United States you might be interested in."

"How do you know about problems in the US?"

"Because they start here in France."

Raven took another drink. "I'm listening."

"My boss, Abelard Joulbert, is marked for death if the government keeps up the crackdown. The syndicate has already lost millions of dollars, and the bosses are blaming him for not having enough control over the authorities. He has a contact in San Francisco, a man named King, and they are going to join forces to get cocaine into the US and make up for the losses."

It wasn't the first attempt at a "French connection" in the United States. French drug runners had been getting greedy of late, no longer satisfied with France's unending appetite for narcotics. They'd branched out to Australia in recent months and attempted to subvert well-oiled drug machines in Central America as well. Anything to extend their empire. Raven knew of one particular disaster in Northern Ireland where French narcotics traffickers ran afoul of the Real IRA, who monopolized the territory. A lot of French drug runners died in the clash. The defeat was so brutal the northern counties were now off-limits. French kingpins wanted nothing to do with them.

"Old Abelard sounds desperate," Raven said.

"Yes. King is a syndicate boss with his own problems, which is why Joulbert reached out. If this deal falls through, my boss and the American are getting the axe. Literally."

"Maybe it *should* happen," Raven said.

"But if they are successful—"

"What do you know about the American, this Mr. King?"

"Nothing, only his name."

"First name?"

"No. He's in San Francisco."

"Enough for a start." Raven pulled a wad of paper notes from a pocket. He peeled off four, paused, and a fifth, and passed them to Dimitri. Dimitri stashed the money in his shirt pocket.

"Get out of here, Dimitri. I'd hate to see anything happen to you."

"I'm already being watched."

Raven frowned. "Why?"

"Joulbert suspects us all of ratting to the police. In his sweep of our ranks, he's killed people because of suspicion. If they find out I'm talking to you—"

"Were you followed here?"

"At first. I lost them."

"You sure?"

"I hope so."

Raven sighed and scanned the room. None of the patrons seemed out of the ordinary, and nothing had tripped his mental alarms when he arrived. If assassins lurked within the crowd, he'd deal with them. They wouldn't make a move until they could make the kill and get away clean. Fighting their way through a half-drunk hysterical crowd wasn't good strategy.

Raven ate his second olive, savoring the taste, and downed the rest of the martini in two long swallows.

He put another bill on the bar. "For yours and mine. I'm leaving. Give me ten minutes and come out."

"Thank you, Sam."

"Change your ways, Dimitri. I don't want to see you again unless you're selling popcorn at an amusement park."

Raven slid off the stool and made for the rear exit.

The fresh garbage smell in the back alley hit Raven smack in the face. He turned right, reaching the busy sidewalk, and walked with the flow to the next corner. He turned right again, and found an alcove near the bar entrance. He put his back to the hard brick and felt their rough texture through his jacket.

He remained in the shadow of the alcove, watching real life pass by. He sighed. So much of his own life was spent in the shadows, watching. He had his reasons, reasons branded deep into his soul, represented by the locket around his neck. He never opened the locket or spoke about what might be inside.

It served as a reminder of what he lost, and what he fought for. For anybody else, it would have been a millstone; for Raven, the locket provided motivation.

Presently Dimitri exited with car keys jangling in his hand. He turned left, passing Raven. Raven let out a whistle to let Dimitri know he was nearby. He watched for sharks, the two-legged variety who often carried guns. Unlike sharks, they weren't hard to kill.

If Dimitri had not always come through with good intelligence, Raven might not have lost any sleep should he get whacked by his own people.

But he had been reliable. He'd put his neck on the line for Raven's crusade against the world's predators many times. Raven owned him something in return.

He spotted the sharks.

Two men leaning against a battered Peugeot on the other side of the two-lane street. They talked loudly and smoked cigarettes and when they saw Dimitri, they tossed the cigarettes in the street. One man climbed behind the wheel of the car while the other ran across the street. He held his hand out to stop the flow of traffic, ignoring indignant horn blasts.

"Dimitri!" the man called.

The Peugeot merged into traffic, but a stoplight delayed the driver. Thug One reached the sidewalk and fell in step with Dimitri.

Raven left the alcove. He moved around other pedestrians who were too focused on their night out to notice the deadly play unfolding in front of them.

He closed in on Dimitri and Thug One as the goon put a hand on Dimitri's shoulder and pushed him toward an alley entrance.

Raven did not want to use his .45. He lived by certain rules, and one of those was no gunfire in public, unless a greater threat forced him to break the rule. His job was to make sure the threat didn't materialize. The enemy didn't always make it easy, and it helped to strike before they had a chance to endanger innocent people.

He palmed a leather sap from the right pocket of his sport coat and reached the alley. He heard a fist strike flesh with a sharp crack.

Raven's shoes scraped on cement as he turned into the alley. Dimitri, crying out, hit the ground hard, his bulk making him look like a beached whale. Thug One prepared to kick at Dimitri's thick belly.

Raven swung the sap. The leather tip, stuffed with lead shot, smacked against Thug One's right shoulder.

The goon yelled, pivoting, trying to sidestep as Raven lashed out again. The sap banged into his chin, stunning the man, and Raven lashed out with a spin-kick, striking him in the center of his chest. Thug One rocketed into the wall with a thud and slid onto his bottom and passed out.

Raven twirled the sap in the air, caught it, and returned it to his pocket.

Dimitri, on hands and knees, started to rise. "Another I owe you."

"I'm only getting started." Raven grabbed Thug One and hoisted his bulky body across his shoulders. He grunted under the man's weight. "You need to drop a few pounds, fatso."

"Me?" Dimitri said.

Raven grunted. "Not you, but if the shoe fits and all that."

"Yeah, yeah." Dimitri brushed off his clothes.

Raven left the alley and stepped onto the street. Cars jerked to a halt, more horns blaring. Raven ignored them as he approached the Peugeot, stuck like the other cars. He smiled at the driver, turned his back to the car, and dropped Thug One on the hood with a shrug. Thug One's body banged loudly, the metal hood bending with the force.

The driver scrambled to get out a gun from under his coat. Raven spun around and pumped his fist into the open window to strike the driver's face once, twice. Two devastating blows. The first punch snapped the driver's nose out of place; the second split skin near his left cheek. As the driver recoiled with a scream, Raven grabbed the man's gun and tossed it into the rear seat.

"Be seeing you," Raven said.

He continued to the other side and hurried along the sidewalk. The action had been too fast for passersby to capture on a cell phone, but there were CCTV cameras to look out for. Such was modern life. He didn't want to end up on YouTube.

There was no sense in sharing another goodbye with Dimitri. He'd said all he was going to say to the man who wanted out of the criminal life. Dimitri was on his own now, and Raven had other priorities. He needed to return to his hotel and book the first available flight out of France. There were two syndicates to smash, two kingpins who needed killing. He might be able to take down both with one shot. It was the perfect mission. Maximum disruption, maximum casualties. The kind of battle he lived for.

Everything else had long ago been taken from him.

CHAPTER TWO

It was too cold to sit outside. The chilly breeze off the Golden Gate was welcome in the hot summer; now, in winter, it was a curse. And today it wasn't a breeze, it was a strong wind, and it rattled the glass panes.

Dixon King sat on a white leather couch in front of a wall-mounted big screen LCD display. To his left, through a wall of windows, a patio overlooked the ocean and the Golden Gate Bridge stretched into San Francisco. Heating and cooling the place was expensive. He changed out the windows and seals biannually to make sure he wasn't losing hot or cold through any cracks. He didn't feel like doing the math to see if he was saving money, breaking even, or spending more. He didn't have to. He had enough. He made more money while sleeping than most people did in their entire lives.

The magnificent view was the reason he'd bought the 23-milllion-dollar home in Marin County, but half the year he couldn't be on the patio without a parka. Sometimes it amused him. Most of the time it didn't. Winter was the time where he felt he'd wasted his money and should have picked out a place in the city.

But he also knew the home in Marin provided an escape

from the city's congestion. Living in a sea of buildings could stifle the spirit of any man. He'd worked hard for the privilege and intended to exercise all options now available.

He hadn't always had such luxuries.

But King wasn't the only one who felt choked by steel and glass, and understood why most workers commuted to San Francisco, and exited when the clock struck five o'clock, or whatever time the civilians ended their day to go home to families and housework and television. He had no idea what their lives were like. They had no idea what his was like. Just as it should be.

The exterior and interior of the house was white, with polished white marble accented with gold sparkles throughout. King liked white, the color symbolized purity. His business was a dirty one, and he liked having a sanctuary that suggested his entire life didn't wallow in the mud.

King sat in a blue silk kimono with his hair still wet. Mid-60s with gray hair, but trim and muscular, his focus was on the television news. The bottle-blonde anchor, her face caked with makeup to hide the fact that she was north of 50, reported:

"The San Francisco Coroner will release the autopsy on the death of District Attorney Dan Whitlow tomorrow. Mr. Whitlow died two weeks ago in a South of Market apartment near UCSF. Paramedics were summoned to the apartment around two a.m. and found Whitlow unresponsive. Attempts to revive him failed, and they pronounced him dead at the scene..."

While the woman talked, B-Roll showed the late Dan Whitlow in public, with his pretty wife, and in court, where he behaved like a Roman gladiator taking on one opponent after another. The anchor continued:

"Whitlow was also known for his aggressive prosecution techniques against drug offenders, but he had a passionate belief in prison rehabilitation."

The screen cut to old interview footage of Whitlow, in a blue suit/black tie combo, hair slicked back, his movie-star face bright under the studio lights.

"The worst part of my job," Whitlow said, "is seeing the same offenders come through the system again and again. It's not enough to put criminals away. We have to *retrain* them while we have the opportunity, and make sure they re-enter society as changed men."

King laughed.

The anchor returned: "San Francisco police continue to not speculate on the cause of death. Whitlow was known to have a heart condition."

Dixon King turned off the sound as the news continued. He clapped his hands. "That's how you kill a man!" he yelled to nobody.

Somebody entered the room.

"Sir?"

King turned his head. His house guard, Wayne, one of his younger staffers, stood in the arched entry way to the living room.

"Is Leo here?"

"Yes, sir."

"Send him in, we're celebrating."

King used his remote to re-wind the news report.

Leonard Wexler, dressed in black, looked like a walking brick wall. His six feet and Marine haircut made him stand out anywhere. Thick muscles bulged through his sport jacket and his polo. Midway through his 40s, he was King's number two in command and King's enforcer. He did most of his work on the streets and displayed a gruff and intimidated demeanor. He had the power to back up the image with sudden violence.

But the power King held, as the man in charge of the overall machine in San Francisco, accomplished more. They balanced each other and had a long history. Both men spent their teenage years in the same New York City street gang.

Wexler stepped into the sunken living room and stood beside the couch.

"Have a chair, Leo. Is this great news or what?" King played the news report again.

"We have a problem."

"I told you to sit."

"You'll be sending me out of here in a minute to deal with the problem, Dixon. No time to sit."

King paused the report. He glared at Wexler. "We got rid of a problem two weeks ago, and everybody's doing what they've been told. Tomorrow the coroner puts out the report we're telling him to release. Then we focus on the election and get our candidate into the DA's office. No more problems. Now we have a new one?"

"The hooker freaked out."

King's face blanched. He blinked.

Wexler continued. "She's gone to the cops."

"This," King said, "is not something we can tolerate."

Dixon King and his agreement with the French syndicate depended on a friendly face in the top offices of city law enforcement. The DA was their first target.

Dan Whitlow might have been a crusader with a touch of bleeding-heart progressive, but he had his weakness. He liked hookers and cocaine. Despite his heart condition, he snorted as much snow as he could, and counted on medication to keep his ticker working. He might as well have died from refusing to listen to his doctor as he had anything else.

King and Wexler had concocted the plan to dose Whitlow with enough cocaine to put him out of their misery. They'd found a hooker to do the job and gave her a lot of money to make sure Whitlow put the stuff up his nose in a timely manner.

King figured a nobody like the hooker would do the job and vanish, but now he realized his error.

"We should have whacked the bitch before Whitlow reached the morgue," King said.

"We still can."

"You think?"

"Our friend at the cops' headquarters delivered the news, so he's going to keep us advised."

"Okay."

"But—"

"What?"

"We're going to have to get rid of her and any statement she makes. Who she talks to is out of our control. It might get bloody."

King sighed and glanced at the frozen picture on the television. "We tried not being bloody. Now we get bloody. That's your job, Leo."

"Of course."

"You're right, you had no time to sit. Get going."

Wexler nodded and exited the living room. His powerful strides echoing across the marble hallway floor.

King turned off the television with a grunt of disgust.

The wind outside rattled the windows once again.

San Francisco SWAT Sergeant Patrick Jensen, "Trick" to his friends and colleagues, watched Inspector Kayla Blaine interview a hooker.

It wasn't the flashiest of assignments. Trick had to admit there was nothing flashy about his police career overall, but one of his jobs was protecting high-risk witnesses. Tonight, he was guarding a hooker who had information on the supposed murder of the San Francisco District Attorney.

The Dan Whitlow story had gripped the city for the previous two weeks. The official position of the city was mourning a fallen law enforcement veteran, but it wasn't hard to find cops who felt indifferent. Whitlow had flaunted the laws he'd pledged to uphold with his coke and hooker habit. It was a whispered secret, not known to the public, but plenty of cops knew the score.

Whitlow wasn't the first law enforcement officer to bend the rules, and he wouldn't be the last. It was a fact of life Trick didn't like but had to live with. Too many people in positions of power liked their vices. The problem was other cops, seeing the easy pickings of a culture of corruption, fell into the same traps. They spent their careers protecting graft more than citizens.

The only thing a good cop could do was his or her best and get out with pension intact. He knew it was Kayla Blaine's goal as well. She was one of the good cops.

Trick stood in a corner of the living room in a nondescript house in Colma, south of San Francisco. The SFPD used the home for such meetings. The house was in an isolated neighborhood near Highway 1, close to the coast. They were far apart enough from neighbors for the comings and goings not to be noticed.

The brass brought in Kayla because the hooker swore she'd only tell her story to another woman. Trick didn't blame her. She'd have been interviewed by a woman anyway, per department standards, to avoid the risk of any of the guys trying to take advantage of her. It had happened before. Another fact of life Trick accepted with disgust.

Kayla and the hooker sat at the kitchen table, going through their preliminary questions. Who are you, why are you talking to the police, the usual warm-up. It was the start of a long night, maybe a couple of nights. Trick had no idea how much the hooker knew, or how long she'd take to tell her story.

Four other male SWAT officers like Trick, all armed, were spread around the house. Only a select few in the Southern Division, responsible for the area of the city where Whitlow died, knew of the interview. The DA's death had conspiracy written all over it because of the gag order placed on all officers. The city didn't want anybody talking about what happened. Rumors spread regardless, because Whitlow was in an apartment not his, with a woman not his wife, and left alone either before or after he died.

Paramedics had found evidence of a woman being in the house with him, a glass stained with lipstick. Partial prints matched the witness's, so they knew her story had credibility. She wasn't a crank looking for a way off the street for a couple of nights.

If somebody had wanted Dan Whitlow dead, the same somebody might want the hooker dead. Trick wasn't naive, he knew how the city worked, and who pulled the strings. If whoever killed the DA might also plan a hit on the house, Trick wanted to make sure they died trying.

One thing distracting Trick from the boredom was the women themselves. They couldn't tell he was looking. Or maybe leering was the word. They weren't hard to look at, especially Kayla, but the hooker held even more mystery. She was in her 20s, might have been a college student, with a husky figure and attributes she couldn't conceal even under her big sweatshirt.

Kayla was equally attractive, a little older than the hooker, with long black hair and a fit runner's body. She ran the Bay to Breakers race each year but had yet to come in at first place.

He took a deep breath and let the conversation before him continue, a silent witness to the proceedings, almost a ghost. If the women knew he was there, they betrayed no knowledge of his presence.

Homicide Inspector Kayla Blaine had certainly had better assignments, but part of her skill set was getting nervous witnesses to talk.

She said, "Tell me your name."

Her voice was soft, her tone low, comforting. The young woman across the table from her had big brown eyes and looked scared. She'd seen something bad, and Kayla had to get her to reveal the knowledge. Along with a notepad, she had a digital recorder between them to capture the conversation.

"Margot," the hooker said.

"Last name?"

"Do you need it?"

"We need it, hon. It's OK. You're protected. See all these guys around here?"

The woman's brown eyes darted over Kayla's shoulder. She appeared to have not noticed the guards before, but only because she had so much on her mind. Witnessing a murder could make one preoccupied indeed. She looked at Kayla. "Hensley," she said.

"Where are you from?"

"Vermont."

"How long have you been an escort?"

Margot laughed. "We're using that word?"

Kayla Blaine didn't offer a reply, but instead waited for Margot to answer. Not insulting a witness was a great way to break down barriers.

"Two years," Margot said.

"All right." Kayla hesitated. She didn't like this job. It was bad enough the DA was dead; now she had to pry into his private life. It was none of her business who somebody slept with, how they accomplished the task, or even if they paid for it. Yeah, there were laws against prostitution; she'd enforced those laws for as long as she could remember. But only because she had to. Had she had her own way, women like Margot wouldn't be prosecuted for what they did, and neither would their clients. There were worse crimes to occupy the attention of police. Somebody paying for sex shouldn't have been one of them.

Kayla was the only member of her family to join the police force, something her father didn't approve of, had never warmed to, and continued to speak against. He'd wanted her to pick a normal career, a 9-to-5, something boring but stable. Above all, she knew, he didn't want her in danger, which she appreciated, at least. Parents worry about their kids, and she was giving her parents something to worry over all the time. It was one of the reasons she'd picked San Francisco, leaving her family in Connecticut. To succeed, she had to be far away from them.

Her desire to enter law enforcement stemmed from not wanting a normal career. She wanted to *do* something with her life, not waste away in a cubicle wondering if she was made for something bigger. If the cops didn't work out, if The Job proved to be too much, she could always make a change. But instead, she shined bright as an officer, moving from traffic to vice and then homicide, achieving the rank of inspector, like Dirty Harry, but she did her work by the book. She liked the Dirty Harry movies, though, and had a boxed set of the films in her DVD library. Every cop she knew had them too.

Kayla was well aware of the big man behind her. She'd worked with Trick countless times, felt comforted by his presence, and his skill with the M4 automatic rifle. She picked up a coffee mug and sipped. Margot, she noticed, hadn't touched her coffee. She'd asked for it black while Kayla had added milk and sugar. Kayla liked little treats during long nights.

"Tell me what happened two weeks ago," Kayla said.

Margot hesitated. "Well—"

And the lights snapped out.

Kayla called out, "What's happening, Trick?"

Margot let out a gasp at the obvious alarm in Kayla's voice. She made no move to reassure the young woman as she reached for her pistol.

Trick, on the radio, his deep voice loud in the dark kitchen, called to his SWAT colleagues. "Anybody see anything?"

A crash of automatic weapons fire outside the house was his only answer. The patio doors beyond the kitchen exploded inward.

CHAPTER THREE

Trick snatched up his M4 carbine, bringing the stock to his shoulder. He advanced through the doorway into the kitchen. The light mounted on the forward grip providing illumination.

He didn't need to shout for the women to do something. Kayla grabbed Margot Hensley by the hand and hauled her away from the table. Both squeezed by Trick as he centered his sights on the two entering gunmen.

His finger worked the trigger. There was no hesitation. Both shooters wore black, carrying automatic weapons, their faces uncovered. Trick's first salvo of rapid-succession single-shots found their mark.

One of the gunmen pitched back, spurts of blood sprouting along the center of his chest. His partner didn't waste a minute returning fire. The full auto blast caught Trick in the belly. His tactical vest protected him, but the impact knocked him off his feet onto the tiled kitchen floor. As he tried to regain his feet, a follow up blast from the surviving gunman turned his lights out forever.

Kayla Blaine and Margot Hensley ran toward the front of the house. Kayla neared the door with her .40 caliber SIG Sauer P229 service pistol in hand. The frame splintered as shotgun blasts ripped through the wood.

Margot screamed, pulling away from Kayla's grip. Kayla leveled her pistol at the opening door, firing twice. The SIG Sauer P229 snapped in her hand. She had no idea if she hit anybody. Kayla grabbed Margot and lead her through a laundry room to another door and into the garage.

More shooting from inside, men shouting.

"Hurry," Kayla hissed, keeping her voice low.

The garage had no cars inside. It wasn't used like the rest of the house. A car in a garage was a death trap; all vehicles were outside. Kayla and Margot dashed across the concrete floor to yet another door leading to the side of the house. Kayla checked left, right. No threats. The side gate, part of the fence, was on the right. Kayla flipped the catch and peered out.

If the shooters were all inside, they had seconds to get to a car. Kayla had the keys to her issued car in the pocket of her jeans.

"Head for the silver Ford," Kayla said. "Now!"

The two women ran, Margot in the lead as Kayla scanned for threats. A gunman emerged from the house, using the front doorframe to brace his weapon and take aim. He started to shout an alarm. Kayla blasted a third eye in his forehead to shut him up.

She used the key fob to get the doors to a Ford Fusion unlocked. She hurried to the driver's side. Margot opened her door. Kayla saw the young woman moving, almost in slow motion, especially as another gunner came out. This one didn't waste time talking. Kayla told Margot to get down as she aimed over the roof of the car. Margot was between her and the gunman; her shots had to count.

The gunman fired first.

The blaze of full auto rounds struck the car, rocking the body, shattering glass. Margot Hensley screamed as rounds cut through her. Her body tumbled to the sidewalk. Kayla fired twice, the gunman yelling as a slug tore through his shoulder. As he moved for cover, Kayla jumped into the car and started the motor. She fired out the passenger door as she sped away, the force of her departure slamming the door shut. Window glass tinkled as she peeled out.

She dropped the gun on the passenger seat and drove.

Alone.

No witness.

No protection team.

Somebody betrayed them. Her friends were dead. Whatever Margot Hensley was going to say was lost.

If Margo had been important enough to kill, what secrets had she held?

And who had killed Dan Whitlow?

Another car left the scene of the safe house containing the remaining gunmen. The crew included the wounded man who grasped his left arm to his side. Blood seeped through the fingers of his right hand has he held onto his wound. The policewoman's bullet had ripped through his shoulder. He clenched his teeth tight.

Leonard Wexler, seated on the passenger side, wasn't concerned with the dead or wounded man. They were paid to take risks, and the hit on the SFPD safe house, a rare event, was a risk indeed. He held his automatic rifle between his knees.

But the hit had paid off.

The house, now ablaze, burned brightly in the rearview mirror. The neighbors would be lighting up 911 by now.

The flames would destroy any evidence of value, written or recorded.

Wexler only cared that the mission had been a success.

Well, mostly.

He told the shooter to hang in there, they'd have him fixed up right away. The shooter nodded, his eyes teary, his right hand slick with the blood leaking from his body.

The driver steered the car along a twisty road heading for Highway 1 North. Leo Wexler dialed a number on his cell phone. The mob doctor who could take care of the shooter lived near Crissy Field, close to the Golden Gate Bridge. And if the patient died, they were close enough to the water to chuck him into the bay.

But shoulder wounds weren't usually lethal.

Dixon King answered with a gruff, "What happened?"

"We got the hooker," Wexler said.

"Good."

"We got most of the cops."

"What do you mean by *most*, Leo?"

"The protection detail is dead, but the woman inspector got away."

"How much did the hooker tell her?"

"Not much. She had a notepad and a digital recorder in the kitchen. It's all going up in the fire."

"Doesn't mean Inspector Blaine gets to live, Leo."

"Okay."

"For all we know Margot Hensley said something before the session started. She won't forget anything."

"Understood."

"She *has* to be killed."

"I get it, boss."

"Don't fail. Call our friend and see what he says."

"I'll call him right now."

Wexler ended the call and cursed. Dixon King, his boss, could be a demanding taskmaster.

But maybe he had a point. The hunt wasn't over after all.

Leonard Wexler made another call.

CHAPTER FOUR

"You can't go home, Kayla."

"No kidding, Marty!"

Kayla continued driving, not paying any attention to where she was going. She ignored the cold chill raging in the car from the broken windows. She drove without any destination in mind, making random turns, reversing course when she could. Anything to shake any tails. Her backside looked clear, but how could she know for sure?

Her pulse still raced. She had a hard time catching her breath.

Her boss, Captain Marty Dresnick, at least answered when she called to tell him what happened.

"We have a mole," Dresnick said, "there's no other answer."

"If I can't go home, where do you suggest I go?"

"Don't tell me. This line may be tapped. Surely you know somebody, somewhere you can stay."

An idea formed in Kayla's mind.

"I can think of one or two people."

Only one but Marty didn't need to know.

"Get squared away," Dresnick said, "and I'll start working this end. We'll find out what happened, Kayla, I promise."

"Okay."

"Did the witness tell you anything?"

"Not enough but for a hit like this, you *know* she knew something."

Kayla ended the call with disgust and dropped the phone on the passenger seat next to her SIG Sauer. She wasn't mad at Marty. She'd woken him from a sound sleep; he'd be up the rest of the night and into the morning. She was disgusted because her mission was a total failure. Witness dead. Friends dead. And she was on the run from an unknown enemy who might have shared a desk near her at the Southern Station office.

Kayla finally pulled into a small parking lot at a McDonalds and turned off the car. She sat with her head in her hands, unable to cry, still pumped from the action. She needed a safe-haven and fast.

She grabbed her phone and made another call, this time to a friend from the office.

"Hello?" The woman's voice on the other end was groggy with sleep.

"Lori, it's Kayla. I know it's late, but I need help."

"Kayla?" the sleepy voice said.

"Yes. It's urgent. Trick and his team and my witness are dead."

"*What?*" No more grogginess now. Sergeant Lori Morgan was all ears as Kayla related the story.

"I need to crash at your place."

"Get over here."

Kayla wanted to smile. She knew Lori wouldn't let her down.

"I'll be right over. We have a lot of talk about."

Wexler said into the phone, "Where is she?"

"I have no idea," the mole told him. "She won't go home. I can give you a list of friends she might call, but I'd only be guessing."

"Then guess."

The mole rattled off a trio of names and addresses. Wexler wrote them down on a pocket notebook and hung up. The mole didn't deserve the politeness of a goodbye.

He told the driver to continue to the doctor's place. They wouldn't be working any more tonight. Searching for Kayla Blaine would take a bit more time than the boss might want, but Wexler didn't give a damn. He'd find the woman and leave her in a ditch in his own time.

Kayla Blaine stumbled into Lori Morgan's apartment, still gasping for breath. Lori locked the door.

"Oh, God, Lori," Kayla said.

"Come on. I have wine."

It was late for wine. Or was it early? Kayla needed something to take the edge off and a slug of anything alcoholic seemed like a good fit.

Lori was wrapped in a thick pink bathrobe. She worked out of the Southern Station same as Kayla but was part of the vice squad instead of homicide. They had worked vice together prior to Kayla's promotion to inspector.

She took Kayla into the kitchen, but Kayla reacted to the sight of the table with an audible gasp. She finally began to sob, diving to Lori for comfort. Lori wrapped her arms around Kayla and made soothing sounds while rubbing her back. Kayla sobbed on her shoulder.

They moved to the couch in the living room instead. Lori grabbed the two glasses of wine she'd already poured and handed one to Kayla. Kayla drank the glass faster than intended, but it helped calmed the racing emotions in her head. Lori sat opposite her and asked what had happened.

Kayla gave her fellow cop a full report of the events at the safe house.

When Kayla finished, Lori finally drank some of her wine and set the glass on the coffee table.

"Wow," Lori said.

"Yeah."

Kayla wiped her eyes. Lori grabbed a box of tissues from an end table.

Kayla wiped her eyes and blew her nose. She put the used tissue on the table.

"Can I stay here tonight?" Kayla said.

"The guest room is all set."

"Thanks."

"Does the boss want you in the office tomorrow?"

"I have no idea."

"Get some rest, if you can, and we'll sort this out tomorrow."

Kayla nodded and followed Lori down a short hallway to the guest room. A bed awaited and looked good to Kayla. Her body felt tense, the shock of action still wearing off.

They said goodnight and Kayla shut the door.

She took her holster from the nightstand and pulled out the SIG pistol. She held the gun in her hand and looked at the cold blue steel. Carbon scoring marked the barrel. The rounds she'd fired had done nothing to protect Trick or the other cops. Nor had they protected her witness. She jammed the gun into the leather and returned the weapon to the nightstand.

Sitting on the edge of the bed, she put her head in her hands and let out a long sigh.

Tonight had been a horror show. Worse because the safe

and controlled confines of the safe house had been violated. The department had a traitor in its midst; a traitor had no qualms about killing.

Who?

And why?

CHAPTER FIVE

Sam Raven's fist struck the pusher's face with a loud crack.

The man recoiled with a yelp, his nose broken, blood streaming down the front of his face. He crashed against the alley wall. Raven didn't give him a break. He closed in fast, slamming another hard blow to the man's stomach, his fists protected by leather gloves. The pusher doubled over, retching a little, vomiting a burst of muck on the already dirty ground. Raven shoved the man down, kicked him in the stomach. The pusher folded in half under the blow.

The pusher was young, skinny, wearing street clothes. Sleeve tattoos on both arms, spiked blond hair. He'd been working the street in a two-block radius, selling baggies of cocaine. His customers pulled up to the curb in front and attracted his attention.

It was well past three a.m., the street quiet and free of pedestrians. Raven had the pusher all to himself. Guns were okay to use. He had a bullet nestled in the chamber of the Nighthawk Custom Talon with the pusher's name on metaphorically scrawled on the tip.

Raven wore head-to-toe black, with a black leather jacket. The left pocket bulged from the mini tote bag stuffed within.

Raven kneeled beside the hurt pusher. Blood from his smashed nose dripped onto the concrete. "Sucks, don't it?"

The pusher coughed, trying to curse, the words garbled.

"Get up." Raven grabbed the man's hair, pulling hard, forcing the pusher to his feet. He rose with the man. "I want your stuff."

The pusher, too stunned and hurt to respond, wavered unsteadily.

Raven gave him a shove. "Now!"

The pusher mumbled something about his motorcycle parked deeper in the alley. Raven took out his Nighthawk Custom and jammed the barrel of the custom M1911-style pistol into the man's back. "Walk slow."

The pusher's feet scraped the ground, Raven shoving the man ahead when he stalled. Finally, they reached the Honda Shadow where the pusher opened one of the side containers. He showed Raven the baggies of cocaine inside.

"Nice," Raven said. He pulled the bunched tote bag from the left pocket of his leather jacket and shook it open. The zipper was already undone.

He said, "Fill 'er up."

The pusher found some strength and tried to swing a punch into Raven's gut. It was easy to block. Raven bashed him over the head with the .45 and shoved him to the ground once again.

The pusher groaned and spit blood. He tried to push himself up with his hands. Raven kicked him. "Get on your knees."

The pusher made it to his hands and knees before pausing, breathing through his mouth since his nose didn't work. Raven grabbed the collar of his shirt, hauling his upper body upright.

"Make a lot of money on this beat?"

The pusher didn't respond.

"I bet your boss isn't going to be too happy, right?"

A mumble in reply.

"Too bad."

Raven moved away to avoid blood spatter, aimed behind the pusher's right ear, and squeezed the trigger.

The .45 hollow-point blasted through the pusher's head without resistance, the roar deafening in the confines of the alley. The bullet took off one side of the pusher's face, where it flopped wetly on the ground. The rest of his body fell, the pusher's head landing with a slap.

Raven put his gun away and filled the tote bag with the baggies of cocaine.

Patting down the pusher, he took a wad of cash from a pocket. Raven never had to worry about money. The bad guys always had plenty for him to take. His search also turned up a cell phone, a major score. Checking the contacts, he noted the last number called. Joey Franklin. The street boss. Raven paused long enough to take a picture of the dead man, and a picture of what was inside the tote.

He'd been in San Francisco for several days, scouting the territory, learning the lay of the land. Selecting the pusher as his first target, he'd stuck with the man for a day, identifying his boss. Then he followed the boss, picking up his name and noting *his* routine as well. It might have been easier to go to the street boss directly, but Raven wanted an edge. He wanted the street boss shaken up and out of his comfort zone and ready to respond to Raven's orders.

He made the call as he walked the three blocks to his rented BMW 530i, the cool night air drying the sweat on his face. He didn't feel bad about the killing. He might as well have been swatting a fly for all the reaction he had. Another one down. How many more to go before the innocent no longer suffered?

Joey Franklin, the street boss, answered. "It's late, dummy."

Raven said, "The dummy is dead."

"Who is this?"

"The guy who killed your dummy."

"What do you want?"

"It's not what I want," Raven said, "it's what you want."

"You gonna talk some sense?"

"I'll make it simple. I killed your man and now I have your product. If you want me to return the item, it's going to cost you."

Silence followed by a bluster of threats, curses, the usual routine. Raven gave him a minute and said, "You done?" when the street boss finally paused.

"You're the man now," Franklin said.

"You have a warehouse I saw you visit." Raven said. He gave the location.

"Yeah, it's mine."

"Meet me there in two hours."

"Oh, I'll be there," Franklin said, getting blustery again. "I'm going to leave you with enough holes in you for sense to leak in, and I'm stuffing your body in a barrel and drop you in the bay."

"Can't wait. Oh, and I'm sending a couple of pictures. Bye."

Raven sent the two pictures in a text message and dropped the cell down a gutter. When he reached his rental, he drove to the warehouse.

Sam Raven blended with the shadows once again.

He lay on an upper catwalk leading to a raised office overlooking the floor. Crates with various labels stenciled across the wood packed the floor. The contents of the crates didn't matter to him. They were various items of contraband controlled by the local drug thugs.

Raven breathed easy, the tote bag of cocaine beside him.

The Talon pistol rode under his left arm, but he'd brought

additional armament. Smuggling weapons in the X-ray proof bottoms of his suitcases had become so easy he barely thought of the process any longer. The CIA had taught him the trick, and the first few times his movements required bringing his own weapons, he'd nearly sweated through his clothes wondering if security would find the hardware. They never did. Now on his own, he'd continued the practice, and remained absolutely calm while doing so.

His CIA days were long behind him.

As were many other things.

What was important to him was now and how best to take advantage of his early arrival.

Engines outside. Multiple cars pulling up. He checked his watch. Still thirty minutes before the scheduled time, and he grinned. They wanted to be early. Tough luck on them. He'd been even earlier. If you show up last to a meet, you get left behind. The CIA had taught him that, too.

A door opened, the exterior light bulb outside spilling across the warehouse floor. Shadows filled the light. Somebody in command barked orders, and three men followed the light trail inside.

Three inside. How many outside?

Joey Franklin, the street boss, was thick in the middle, bald, and liked to talk. He told the two gunmen with him to spread out while he lit a cigarette. If killing the drug runners had been his goal, Raven could have popped all three and been gone before their bodies hit the floor. But the head thug probably had information Raven needed. *Information* was the goal of the night. If he left any bodies behind, so much the better. Icing on the cake.

The gunmen, toting submachine guns, hid among the crates. Their boss paced and blew clouds of smoke. Three cigarettes later, a haze hung in the air, and the time of the meeting had arrived.

Raven didn't move.

Ten minutes passed.

"Where is this guy?" the boss demanded to nobody in particular, agitated now.

Raven grinned. He yelled, "Above you!"

The boss snapped his head to the upper catwalks, the two gunmen emerging as well.

"Come out and talk to me," Franklin said.

"You're not giving the orders tonight, fatso."

"Who do you think you are? You blast one of my guys, and have the balls to ask me to come and buy back what's already mine?"

"It's easy money."

"Come down here!"

Raven shifted to bring his primary weapon into his shoulder. The Colt M4 Commando carbine was part of the AR family, chambered in 5.56mm with a barrel length of eleven-and-a-half inches. Perfectly compact, easy to maneuver in tight spaces, and plenty of punch with a 30-round magazine locked in place. An Aimpoint red dot optic sat on top of the gun, with the rear iron sight folded down.

From the muzzle of the M4 Commando extended a custom-made suppressor.

The two gunmen made great targets.

Raven triggered one three-round burst, the action clicking louder than the phuts from the suppressor, brass tinkling on the walkway beside him. The first gunmen cried out as he took all three shots high in the chest, toppling over. The second gunman reacted with shock as he watched his dead friend fall with no idea where the rounds came from. Raven took him down next, another three-shot burst punching through his neck and face.

The boss raised his arms.

"I got no gun! You came here to talk!"

Raven shoved the tote bag off the catwalk, and it landed on the warehouse floor with a thud.

"There's your stuff."

"What do you want?"

The yelling had to attract the attention of the shooters outside, but Raven figured they wouldn't enter until the boss called for them. He rose and moved left, staying near the wall. He kept the muzzle of the M4 Commando trained on the big boss who didn't look so big any longer.

"Tell me about the Frenchman," Raven called out.

"The *who*?"

"You work for Dixon King, right?"

"If you know about this warehouse, you already know the answer, mystery man."

"Tell me about his French buddy, the one coming over to form an alliance. Surely you street dealers gossip."

Raven kept moving, slowly, so the big boss didn't pick up the direction of his voice. A set of steps lay to his right, about ten yards away.

"You want his name or something?"

"I want to know if he's here. I want to know if he's talked with Dixon King yet."

"I have no idea," the big man said, still looking up but turning his face to try and spot Raven's location. "I know a puny shit like you isn't going to stop anything. We're going to have the kind of protection nobody can beat."

"Who said I wanted to stop anything?" Raven said. Almost to the steps now.

"You want to join up? This is a lousy way of introducing yourself, whoever you are."

"We like to get attention," Raven said. He stopped at the

steps and crouched.

"Well, you got mine," Franklin said, "and now you're going to get yours. Do it!"

Lights snapped on, bulbs coming to life in each corner of the building, including the catwalk. The brightness bathed Raven and revealed his position.

But what worked for his enemies also worked against them.

He flicked the M4 Commando's selector switch to full auto with the flick of his right thumb. The street boss started to laugh as he drew a pistol; he never raised the weapon. The carbine chattered a full salvo of 5.56mm rounds. The boss's body fell in a heap, his big belly sticking out like a speed bump, his pistol skidding across the floor.

More shooting started as the gunners from outside joined the fight. Four of them, guns at full volume, and the slugs smacked into the catwalk where Raven had been. Raven hustled down the steps to a landing, changing magazines as he moved. He crouched, scanning for targets. The shooters were moving between the stacked crates. One ran out of sight and footsteps suggested he'd found a way to the top, same as Raven had.

Raven shouldered the Colt and fired a burst. The top of one gunner's head vanished in a spray of red and chunks of skull.

One gunner broke from the crates, running briefly across the open space. Raven fired but missed.

More pounding footsteps on the walkway, approaching fast. Raven snapped his aim to the walkway. A shooter ran toward him, stopping to take aim and fire. His shots went wide, smacking the wall behind Raven.

Raven's return burst punched through the man's stomach, another burst clipping a shoulder. The gunner tipped over and landed below, crashing onto the top of a crate before coming to rest on the floor.

Grabbing the handrail to his right, Raven vaulted over, bending his knees on landing. A stack of crates shielded him. The lights.

Raven aimed up and started firing single shots, shifting his aim, the lights snapping out. The last two gunners yelled to see where they were in relation to each other. Raven returned his side of the warehouse into semi-darkness. He moved forward through the spaces between the crates. Feet shuffled ahead. He dropped. One of the two gunners rounded a corner and Raven struck with the butt stock of the Colt. As the husky shooter fell, Raven followed up with a double tap, two fast shots, to the center of his chest.

He crouched again, peering around the crate. Across the warehouse floor, where the other crates were, the last gunman waited. Between him and the shooter was the exit. If Raven ran for the door, he'd be exposed.

Raven triggered a full auto burst, burning through the magazine, splintering the crates. The man let out a yell, either from being hit or startled by the mass of wood splinters raining on him.

Raven slung the Colt carbine and took out his pistol. Bent at the waist, he made a break for the open floor, keeping his eyes forward. The shooter fired over the top of a crate, Raven diving forward into a somersault. The rounds smacked the ground. Raven came up on one knee and fired the .45 twice. The gunman ducked and shifted, and in doing so briefly exposed a foot and ankle. Raven fired again, one shot, on target. The gunman's scream meant the .45 ACP hollow-point struck home.

Raven made the door, crashing through, rolling forward, coming up in a crouch. He scanned for another target. None presented themselves. Raven sprinted forward. He'd left his car around the corner.

He achieved his goal for the night. The Frenchman was in San Francisco and the plan for the US-France alliance was underway. He didn't have time for a lengthy operation. The alliance had to be stopped *now*, not later.

As an added bonus, he'd left a few dead drug thugs behind with a tote bag full of coke. The police wouldn't be concerned with dead drug dealers, but Raven had a feeling they wouldn't be the last to die. If he left enough bodies on the ground, the cops might wonder who put them there.

Dixon King and his French contact, Abelard Joubert, might ask the same thing.

Raven counted on it.

He sped away, removing a leather glove to wipe his sweaty face as he steered. He smiled despite the narrow escape. He never entered a city quietly. San Francisco had been no different. Now to keep up the pressure...

CHAPTER SIX

Dixon King stood in front of the wall-length mirror and tightened his tie. He'd chosen a blue suit, white shirt, black tie for the day.

The morning outside was crisp and cool. No wind yet. Through his open window, the cooing of pigeons assembled on his rear deck served as an odd soundtrack. He hated pigeons. They were nothing more than flying rats. At least they weren't as bad as the seagulls who limited their foraging activities to the beaches.

There was still no sign of Inspector Kayla Blaine, but she'd turn up. They'd have to carefully remove her because the mess at the safe house had stirred up a hornet's nest. Because of its isolation, and location in Colma, not San Francisco, the incident was being passed off as a house fire. The news of the dead cops had been hushed up. The bodies could keep in the morgue for a short time, but eventually even King knew they'd have to be dealt with in some way. He wasn't blind to reality. By the time he let the city make an announcement about the dead, he'd have suggestions.

He had men all over the city looking for Kayla Blaine. His mole at the Southern Station headquarters was also keeping his eye out.

His attention was partially tuned to the news at the moment. The small flat screen on the wall facing his bed played the morning program on KPIX. Information about District Attorney Dan Whitlow's death continued to filter in. King's contacts planted some of the information. They were already doing more than King had hoped. Lining pockets of the willing, and threatening the families of the unwilling, kept him in control.

"The city coroner's preliminary report," the anchor said, "shows District Attorney Dan Whitlow died from heart failure, with a large amount of alcohol in his system..."

King smiled at his reflection.

"Perfect," he said to himself. The case would be quickly closed, Whitlow buried with honors. City officials would make speeches at his funeral for the need for law-and-order. For future leaders to follow Whitlow's example, and without a hint of irony. King would have a good laugh. Business as usual would continue.

King traveled downstairs to the kitchen, acknowledging guards here and there. The chief house guard, Wayne, was off for the day.

King had no family. The syndicate was his life. Not marrying had been a conscious decision. He'd seen too many others, like him, reach the top only to be foiled by family members who turned rat. He worried enough about lieutenants getting ideas about taking the big chair. He didn't need to wonder about a wife and kids too.

If King wanted a woman, there were plenty available. Most weren't worth the trouble. He only kept them around for a few hours at a time and, so far, the habit had suited him. He paid for their time or he didn't, depending on his mood. The best part of the transaction was when they left.

King went down a flight of curving stairs to the first floor of the house and crossed the entry way to his den. Seated outside the open room, legs crossed, and arms folded, was Leonard Wexler.

"Good morning," Wexler said. He looked tired.

"Late night?" King said as he entered through the arch in the wall, easing behind his desk.

"We had to take care of one of the guys who got shot last night."

"Did he die?"

Wexler shook his head.

"I heard from the coroner," Wexler continued as he followed his boss and stopped in front of the desk.

King eased into the big leather chair. "It's on TV. Nothing was said we didn't want to get out."

"It almost didn't happen," Wexler said. "I got a call this morning—"

"*Another* problem, Leo?"

Wexler nodded. "There's a reporter who says he has proof the coroner is lying."

King cursed and rubbed his forehead. He hadn't even had breakfast yet and he had fires to put out. "Who?"

"Newspaper man named Charles Kline."

King rested his elbows on the armrests of his chair. "Never heard of him."

"Writes for the Chronicle. Normally he works the general assignment stuff, but he's making noise with his editor. So far, the editor knows which side his bread is buttered on and is blocking the story. But Kline went around town last night, talking. A lot. Our people caught him at a bar trying to interest the editor of the Examiner to take the story."

King scoffed. The Examiner, once a newspaper of note, had been reduced to an also-ran tabloid nobody took seriously. Editorial policy was to undermine any official statement coming out of City Hall. They wanted to fight the system and refused to cooperate with King's influence. Whacking a bunch of newspaper people hadn't been on the agenda. A whisper campaign to marginalize their work had been effective instead.

The Examiner's owners insisted on keeping San Francisco a "two newspaper town". Having the Chronicle as the city's newspaper of record wasn't good enough, so its existence continued despite the mockery. King made the owners bleed money to keep the paper going by making sure advertisers remained nervous about placing ads.

"Uh-huh," King said.

"What would you like to do with him?" Wexler said.

"We managed to keep the hooker's killing wrapped tight," King said, "but if we off this guy, we'll be taking a chance we can't afford. Whitlow is almost a memory. But there has to be another way. What exactly is he saying?"

"The coroner's initial report noted the amount of cocaine he ingested."

"The idiot noted that?"

"Yup. I don't know if he wanted an insurance policy or something. I'm going to ask him. But he made those notes, set it aside, and did the report he was supposed to write. Somebody else found the original."

King cursed. "It means whoever found the original leaked it to Kline."

"Yup."

"The coroner have any idea who?"

"I haven't talked to him yet."

"I'd like it if he can find out who did it."

"I'll tell him," Wexler said.

"Remind him we've got his nuts in a vice if he argues. I don't like him trying to step out on us."

"I'll tell him," Wexler repeated.

"Tell him *hard*."

"Yes, sir."

"If this reporter says he has a piece of paper from the coroner's office," King said, "and he got it from an unknown source. Sounds like conspiracy to steal city property."

"You're reading my mind, boss."

"Good." King snapped back the left cuff of his jacket and shirt to check his gold Rolex Sea Dweller. "It's a quarter to eight. Let the cops know. Make some noise. Throwing Kline in a cell isn't a bad idea. I want cameras in front of his house, and I want him thrown into a police car like a side of beef. Make sure he's arraigned in front of one of our judges. It'll show anybody who might play games, like the *coroner*, who still has the power in this city. We'll impress our French friends as well."

"All right," Wexler said. He waited, pressing his lips together.

King frowned. "Something else on your mind?" the boss said. "You got a look on your face."

"We lost some guys last night."

"At the safe house?"

"No, some of our street dealers."

"Tell me more."

"Joey Franklin and some of his guys were killed at their warehouse."

"He one of our dealers?"

"North Beach area, yeah."

"What did the police find?"

"One survivor. Nothing happened to the crates. The shooter left a tote bag full of cocaine and enough brass to make it look like somebody fought a war there."

"Somebody killed our guys and left the drugs and guns?"

Wexler nodded. "The drugs were taken off one of Franklin's

street dealers, who was also killed. Forty-five slug behind the ear. Kid was *executed*. Story is somebody called Joey and offered to sell it back. He also wanted to know about Joulbert."

King frowned.

"I'm already trying to find out who did it."

King nodded. "At least we didn't lose the guns."

But keeping the guns in the crates wasn't much of a victory, and he was now preoccupied with the news. He dismissed Wexler with a short wave and watched his number two exit.

He leaned forward on his elbows and let out a breath. The warehouse news sure sucked the feeling of achievement out of his system. The coroner and the reporter, Kline, could be dealt with easily enough. He had a few days before the first meeting with Joubert and the other Frenchmen.

They were in the city, and initial greetings had happened, but he wanted the crew to take a few days' rest to get over jet lag. He wanted them fresh and alert when business talks finally began in earnest. As an extra precaution, he had a crew watching them.

The crew had picked them up from SFO after taking some discreet pictures now sitting in King's home office safe. He wanted them watched in case they met with anybody else to try and pull a double-cross. He'd been around long enough not to take the chance of letting them run without a leash.

He didn't need any trouble with his operations, from within or without. Problems might make those discussions tougher, so problems needed to be solved before anybody questioned King's ability to follow through with his end.

The syndicate honchos in New York City were counting on Dixon King to solidify the alliance and get drugs flowing up and down the Pacific Coast. He had military weapons stored at several warehouses in the city for the next phase. They'd be moving into new areas, and the competition might not take kindly to the intrusion. Those who refused to join needed to die.

King had to deliver. He'd sold the alliance to his bosses in New York City, who were skeptical at first, but soon bought into the plan. The alliance would generate billions in drug sales. They added one caveat. If King failed, he'd find himself tossed down a bottomless pit. Dixon King had no intention of ending his career in such a fashion. He intended to end his career on his *own* terms.

He had to make sure the election for the new DA went his way, find out who killed his guys, and secure the deal with the French.

He laughed. He was getting up there in years. This would be his greatest knock over ever. He'd started small with a few bank robberies, and now, at the top of his game, he was going to knock over an entire city.

Raven woke up a little after noon and carefully shaved before stepping into a hot shower. Drying off, he left the bathroom naked and dressed in a Tee-shirt and jeans, finally donning his locket. The locket dangled against his chest, nestled in dark chest hair touched with gray. He ordered a room service lunch. He'd slept beyond breakfast, so his craving for the all-meat omelet on the breakfast menu would have to wait.

He'd selected the Hyatt on the Embarcadero. It was a stone's throw from the bay, but his room didn't have an ocean view. His view overlooked Harrison Street, currently crowded with too much traffic. He'd have to go elsewhere in the hotel to watch the water or take a walk outside. Some fresh air felt like a good idea after the action of the previous evening.

He liked being near the ocean, listening to the crashing of

the waves. The sound brought peace to his mind, where there wasn't often peace at all.

He turned on the news while biting into a perfect medium-rare burger. Juice dripped through his fingers onto the plate. He turned the plate so some of the juice landed on his French fries.

The death of San Francisco's district attorney filled the headlines. Raven watched with curiosity, slowly chewing as he took in the details of the coroner's report. He remembered something the drug thug from the warehouse had said.

We're going to have the kind of protection nobody can beat.

Raven put his burger down, wiped his hands on the cloth napkin provided, folded his arms, and watched.

Whitlow, according to reports, had a tremendous record prosecuting drug dealers, users, and assisting federal agents in San Francisco on anti-drug business. For Mr. Whitlow, the war on drugs was a crusade.

...protection...

...nobody can beat.

The news anchors changed the direction of the story. Whitlow had been involved in a heated race to keep his seat. He faced two newcomers with extensive resumes who wanted the DA chair for themselves.

An idea popped into Raven's head.

He picked up his burger again and thought about the idea.

Somebody, maybe Dixon King, needed Whitlow out of the way. So whack him, blame his heart condition. Put time, money, and a little ballot stuffing behind a preferred candidate who would look the other way on *King's* drug business.

Of the two candidates, which one could King be handling?

Raven had hoped for a quick strike to break the alliance. He hadn't wanted a lengthy counter-operation, but now it looked like he'd be in San Francisco longer than expected. There were more threads to unravel. He'd need more time.

He returned to eating, at ease with the decision. He had finished his lunch with his attention still on the screen when a "Breaking News" banner flashed.

The anchor tossed to a reporter live on the scene of an arrest related to the Whitlow case.

"We're at the apartment of a local newspaper reporter named Charles Kline," the reporter said, "who police say has a portion of the coroner's report on the death of District Attorney Daniel Whitlow. We're expecting to hear from a police spokesperson, but as you can see behind me, Mr. Kline is being arrested..."

The reporter pivoted away from the camera shot. The photographer focusing on the action. Police vehicles sat outside the building with cherry lights flashing. The cops half-dragged a man out of the building. He yelled at the camera.

"They're lying to you!"

And he stopped yelling as two cops pushed him into the back of a patrol car.

Raven pushed his plate away. He'd encountered corruption before, all over the world. *What if...*

The men behind the Machine running the city couldn't kill the reporter, but they could shut him up. And the public arrest served as a warning to anybody else thinking of blowing the whistle on the caper. What normally would have been handled privately, without publicity, now required a spotlight. Kline's information countered the official story. His arrest told anybody he had spoken with to keep quiet or else.

There was a cover up in progress. Raven's idea wasn't so far-fetched after all.

The reporter on the television approached an officer. She asked what was happening. The officer said, "We suspect Mr. Kline of being involved with a conspiracy to steal information from the coroner's office."

"A conspiracy means somebody else was working with him," the reporter said. "Do you have information on a second person involved?"

"We do not."

"What was stolen?"

"We can't say at this time."

Raven turned off the set. He didn't need to hear any more. The set up was too perfect, too well organized. The cops were there because somebody ordered them to the scene with specific instructions. Dixon King wanted Charlie Kline out of the way.

Time to do some more digging. He already knew Abelard Joulbert and his crew were in the city. Now he wanted to find out how the death of Whitlow was connected to the proposed alliance. And he wanted to talk to Charlie Kline and find out what he'd learned.

CHAPTER SEVEN

Charlie Kline, his head down, looking dejected, awaited his turn in front of the judge. He had no attorney, so a public defender spoke for him.

Sam Raven sat in the back with the public spectators and journalists. Raven had traded his jeans and Tee-shirt for a blue suit, red silk tie, and white cotton shirt. Slicking his hair and adding a pair of cheap glasses altered his appearance so the video cameras captured his presence, but not his true features.

The bail hearing was short and to the point. Kline entered a plea of not guilty to the charge of stealing city property. The judge set bail at $500,000, which drew a share of gasps from the reporters, and even Raven blinked in surprise. Kline explained, through the public defender, he had no means to post bail. The judge remanded him to county jail until the time of his trial, setting the date for six months out. A bailiff took Kline away.

Raven remained on the hard bench, legs crossed, arms folded, shaking his head. Another point for a cover up. Keep him in a cell until further notice. Well, he'd have to do something. Charlie Kline may not have been able to afford the bond, but Sam Raven's pockets went deep enough *he* could.

Money was never a problem in Raven's line of work. Bad guys always had large amounts of cash handy. Raven often helped himself, accumulating a reserve. He'd have Kline out of lockup in a few hours. And get some answers out of him.

Raven left the courthouse and found his rented BMW 530i in a nearby paid lot. He'd selected the sedan because of its powerful turbocharged straight six engine. A regular four-banger wouldn't suit his needs. He needed power on demand. The leather interior and fully loaded options didn't hurt either.

It took a few hours to process the paperwork at a bonds-man's office, with Raven representing himself as Kline's new attorney. At the jail he posted the bond, took a startled Charles Kline from custody, and told him to keep his mouth shut. They exited the facility and climbed into Raven's car. Raven tossed his glasses into the back seat where they bounced off the cushion and landed on the floor.

"All right, who are you?" Kline said.

"Is that a thank you I heard?"

Raven glanced at Kline. Late 30s, hair too long, thin and wiry, but muscular enough to look like he could handle himself. He'd be no challenge to somebody stronger and twice his weight. He possessed the youthful idealism necessary to go against the grain, which Raven admired. But if Kline wasn't careful, the attitude would cost him his life.

Kline sighed. "Thank you. What do you want?"

"To keep you from getting killed."

"Who are you?"

"Sam Raven. I'm not a cop or a Fed, but I know a cover up when I see it, and somebody wants you out of the way."

"You're telling me!"

Traffic slowed. Road construction up ahead. Raven rolled down a window.

"So. Sam. Are you actually a lawyer?"

"Nope."

"I'm in no better position than I was an hour ago!"

"You're alive. And if you're smart, you'll stay alive, and get the blazes out of this city. But first you need to tell me what you know and how it connects with Dixon King."

Kline cursed. "How do you know his name?"

"I've only been in town a few days, but I'm a fast learner."

"What do you want to know?"

"Let's start with what you acquired from the coroner's office."

"I could use a drink."

"Great idea. Know a place?"

Kline said he did.

Leo Wexler parked in the alley beside a restaurant named Martha's on Eddy Street. He eased his car close to a dumpster near a sign saying, "No Parking Anytime". Nobody would bother his vehicle. Cops knew who ran the restaurant. They also knew to stay away. If King ever required police presence at the restaurant, he had three or four officers on speed dial.

Martha's Restaurant was a small establishment in a neighborhood of apartments, homes and convenience stores. It served basic American food at a fair price, considering how expensive it was to eat out in San Francisco. Nobody questioned why prices were as low as long as the food was good.

The restaurant served as a front for Dixon King's operations, and he occupied an office in the rear. Since it was used for money laundering, he wasn't interested in making large profits, only small ones to keep the IRS happy. He charged the appropriate city surcharges to fund healthcare for the homeless. There was nothing shady about how the restaurant did business.

Wexler left his car and entered through the alley door with his head bent a little, a lifelong habit. Tall men lived with the constant fear of banging their head on something, usually something hard that didn't kill, but made one wish he was dead. The doorway led to a short hallway ending at the busy kitchen. The delightful smells of the afternoon service tickled his nose. Wexler's preferred menu item was the Philly Cheesesteak. Having originally come from New York, Dixon King knew how to make one properly, and taught the head chef accordingly. One deli Wexler frequented sold their "Philly Cheesesteak" with sliced roast beef and a stack of cheese. It was a good sandwich but wasn't a real Philly by any means.

Wexler stopped midway down the hall and stepped into a small office. Dixon King's restaurant office wasn't as opulent as his home, but it was clean and tidy, with '80s movie posters, properly framed, and a set of shelves full of clutter.

King, still in his suit but with the tie loosened and top button of his shirt undone, set down papers and removed his glasses. "Well?"

Wexler eased into the chair in front of the desk.

"No sign of Blaine anywhere."

"She couldn't have vanished from the face of the earth."

"She's hiding somewhere. We've followed some of her colleagues, checked their places, and she's not staying with any of them."

King rocked in his chair and twirled his glasses. He stared beyond Wexler at a wall ahead of him.

Wexler waited while his boss considered the information. He knew locating Inspector Blaine was only a matter of time. She had to eat. She had to change clothes. If another cop had gone to her apartment to collect personal items, his men might have missed the visit. They weren't miracle workers.

But nobody had turned up at her apartment since they began their rotating watch.

"All right, we need to chill a bit," King said. "We might need all hands on deck regarding whoever shot up our warehouse."

Wexler nodded.

"What about Kline?"

"Couldn't make bail. He's in lockup."

"Maybe a Q&A with him will help us. Maybe he talked to more people than the nimrods at the Examiner."

"I'll go see him," Wexler said.

King put his glasses back on and returned to his paperwork.

Leo Wexler exited the office as quietly as he arrived.

CHAPTER EIGHT

Inspector Kayla Blaine turned off the Ford Fusion.

She was on the third level of the parking garage at the Metronome, a mall/theater on the corner of 4th Street and Mission. She desperately wanted to visit the Mel's Diner across the street for something greasy and comforting, but she had to stay off the street. Even meeting Captain Dresnik, while necessary, was more of a risk than she wanted to take at the moment.

Her friend and colleague Lori Morgan had made an early morning run to her apartment to grab clothes and personal items. They sat in a tote bag on the back seat. She wasn't returning to Lori's. She had her mind set on a hotel across the bay, probably Oakland or Berkeley, where she could continue to lay low while the department sorted out the current issues.

Her pulse raced, throat dry. She'd already downed one water bottle but didn't want to be stuck needing a bathroom, so she left a second bottle untouched in the center console.

She'd been in plenty of scrapes as a cop over the years but being the target of multiple assassins was a new experience. Usually anybody who tried to hurt her was right in front of her, and she'd been able to handle the problem per proper procedure, most of the time with help from other officers.

But now she was alone. She'd never felt so alone in her life.

She looked around, checking her mirrors too. Silent cars sat in almost all available slots, new arrivals discharging eager shoppers, mostly female, who paid no attention to her as they entered the main building. Finally, her cell phone chirped.

"Yes?"

"I'm coming up behind you," said Captain Dresnick.

She looked in the rearview and there he was, in his rumpled suit, casually walking toward the car.

"I see you." She ended the call and popped the locks.

Dresnick opened the passenger door and dropped into the seat.

"Well," he said, letting out a sigh.

"Yeah."

"You okay?"

"Barely."

"It's going to be all right, Kayla."

She smiled and felt part of the weight leave her shoulders. Marty Dresnik was not only her captain, but also a mentor. A veteran homicide detective, he guided the crew with a light touch. He knew what they faced on the street. He knew the challenges better than they did. All he wanted from his people was for them to go by the book, clear cases, make them stick, and move on to the next.

Because there was always a next. Homicide units in the city never rested for long.

His dark hair was going a bit gray, but he wore it graciously. His brown eyes and chiseled jaw gave him almost movie star looks. His suit wasn't anything special, purchased off the rack and altered accordingly.

He was an avid runner, like her, but had been sidelined from any local marathons because of knee surgery. He planned to make the next Bay to Breakers race, and Kayla wanted to run alongside him.

"The car got shot up?" he said.

"When I was getting away, yeah. I had to roll down your window because there isn't much glass left. What do we know?"

"Not enough."

"You're really encouraging, Captain."

"We've managed to keep the shooting at the safe house quiet, for now, but eventually somebody is going to ask how four SWAT cops and a witness got killed and nobody said anything."

"We can talk about it when we solve Whitlow's murder," she said.

"What did the hooker tell you?"

"Her name was *Margot*."

Dresnik tried again with a softer tone. "What did she say?"

"Nothing." Kayla threw up his hands in frustration. "We had *just begun* our conversation when the hit happened."

"She didn't tell you anything?"

"I have her name and where she came from and that she'd been an escort for two years."

"Nothing else?"

"No."

Dresnik faced forward, frowning.

Kayla watched him. She felt her hands shaking. Her voice shook as she asked, "What about—"

"Our end?" He looked at her. "We're interviewing each officer who had a connection to Margot's protection."

"Marty, most of them are dead."

"Somebody knows something. We'll find it."

"Uh-huh."

"You can't give up, Kayla. They kill one of us, they hurt all of us. We're going to get to the bottom of this, I promise."

Kayla let out a breath. "Sure."

"Kayla," Dresnik said, hesitating, "we have spotted surveillance outside your apartment."

"I figured."

"But if you don't know anything—"

"They think I do. They won't stop looking for me."

"Also—"

"What?"

"You didn't hear about Charlie Kline?"

She closed her eyes and put her head against the headrest. "They killed him too?"

"No, arrested. It happened around noon today."

"I've kept the news off."

"Allegedly he stole the coroner's report from the lab."

"Why would he do that?"

"Your guess is as good as mine. The coroner says heart failure."

"Which is what we all figured. Not a report worth stealing."

"I think we should pay him a visit. He told you about Margot, right?"

"Yes, he told me about Margot. He said she told him she was in the apartment when Whitlow died." She looked at Marty again. "Where is he? Maybe he took a statement from her—"

"He's at county. Couldn't afford bail."

"Want me to drive?"

CHAPTER NINE

San Francisco Coroner Edwin Gage looked up from his desk and started to shake.

He'd been the city coroner for over thirty years. His gray hair and the lines on his face were a testimony to his years of looking at corpses. He could handle looking at corpses, no matter how mangled, but the big man filling the doorway made him nervous. Gage feared he wouldn't live long enough to get out in one piece.

Leonard Wexler smiled.

"Hello, Ed."

"Um..."

Wexler entered the office and sat in the chair beside Gage's desk. He smiled.

Gage hid his hands in his lap. He didn't want the enforcer to see them shaking. His eyes didn't leave the big man's face.

"We have something we need to talk about."

"Uh-huh."

"Story is, you made a notation of the drugs in Whitlow's system, and what *actually* killed him."

"Look, I didn't—"

"You didn't mean any harm? Is that it?"

"No! No, no, listen to me." Gage scooted back his chair. He wanted some distance from Wexler, but nothing would stop the big man from launching across to hit him. He knew the big man was going to. He'd have a welt on his face for days after.

"Tell me a good story, Ed."

Gage took a deep breath. Now wasn't the time to feel weak. He had to steady his nerves.

"I couldn't do a false report right away."

"Why not?"

"I had the captain of homicide watching me the whole time!"

"Dresnik?"

"No, President *Trump*. Of *course,* Dresnik!"

"Don't get cute with me, Ed."

"He was watching me. He wanted to see what I found. It's not unusual to have an inspector on a case watch an autopsy. There was no way to tell him to leave."

"And you did your routine, checked all the boxes, made your notes."

"I had to!"

"Uh-huh. Then what?"

"Dresnik left. He didn't say anything."

"He walked out?"

"Well, he said thanks, but nothing else."

"Really."

"I swear, Leo, that's what happened. I had no choice!"

"But you kept the report, Ed."

"Do you know how many assistants I have? I got their eyes on me the whole time, especially with a case as big as Whitlow's. I put the report in my desk."

"And then what?"

"We put Whitlow in the cooler. I had to wait until everybody left before I could do the false report King asked for."

"And the original?"

"I was going to take it home and destroy it."

"Destroy it?" Wexler said.

"What else? You think I'm going to keep it around?"

"But when you went to get it, somebody had beat you to it."

"Yes. Exactly. That's *exactly* what happened."

"Who?"

"Could have been anybody. You going to whack my entire staff?"

"What did I say about getting cute, Ed?"

"There's nothing else I could have done. Nothing, Leo, I swear."

"You could have called."

"We'd be in this position no matter what."

"That may be true, but King isn't happy with you. This makes you look bad. You sure you didn't want an insurance policy for yourself? Something to hold back just in case?"

"I'm too old for that crap."

"Sure, you are."

"Really! You think after all this time, knowing King as I do, I'm going to rock the boat?"

"You want to retire."

"Yes!"

"Well, get this." Wexler left the chair. He leaned forward, putting his hands on the arm rests of Gage's chair, his face inches from Gage's nose.

The coroner shrank back, frightened.

"You pull this crap again, something's going to happen. Want to know what it is?"

Gage's body shook. He didn't blink.

"Are you listening, Ed?"

Gage stuttered his response, but finally croaked out, "I'm listening."

Wexler told him.

Dresnik and Kayla showed their badges to gain access to the jail clerk, who sat behind a wire mesh screen. Where the screen met the counter, a rectangular hole had been cut to allow items to pass through.

A hulking six-footer wearing black exited as they entered. Kayla turned to look at the man. He bent his head a little and slipped out the doorway. She didn't recognize him, but the SFPD was a huge outfit.

Dresnik took the lead. He identified himself to the clerk, asking about Charlie Kline. The clerk consulted his battered logbook and said, "Kline made bail, Captain."

"When?"

"Couple hours ago. I told the other inspector the same thing."

"Which inspector?"

"The one you passed, big guy in black?"

"Who signed for Kline?" Dresnik said.

The clerk passed the logbook through the opening. "His lawyer."

Kayla looked at the name. *Samuel Raven.* It meant nothing to her. Dresnik's frown suggested it meant nothing to him as well.

They thanked the clerk and left.

Back in Kayla's car, she began the return trip to the Metronome to deliver Dresnik to his own vehicle.

"Who the hell is Sam Raven?" she said.

"No attorney I've ever heard of, but he might still be legit," Dresnik said. He used his cell phone to search for Raven's name, then put the phone away. "Doesn't appear to be listed in the Bay Area."

"Odd," Kayla said.

But it was a lead. Something to hope for. If Kline was free, and had information to share, he was now in a position to do so, despite whoever wanted to keep him quiet.

Wexler sat in his car, still in the jail parking lot, and made a short report to Dixon King. While he spoke, he watched Kayla Blaine and her captain leave the jail. Had the captain not been present, he'd have made a move to grab her.

"Somebody sprung him."

"He told the judge he couldn't make bail!"

"An attorney posted and signed for him."

"Who?"

"Samuel Raven."

"Never heard of him!"

"I thought I'd look him up and go visit."

"Don't waste time," King said. The boss let out a string of curses. "It's our asses if what we've worked for comes undone!"

"It won't come undone, Dixon."

"It *better* not, Leo. New York will wipe us out. Even you're not strong enough to keep a bullet from splitting open your head."

Wexler glanced at his reflection in the rearview mirror of the car. "I think about that all the time," Wexler said.

"You talk to the coroner?" King said.

Wexler cracked a smile. "Yeah, we talked. He understands the situation."

"What did you tell him?"

"I said if he ever tries to screw with us again, I'd snap off his granddaughter's fingers and wear them as a necklace."

King chuckled. "Good one."

"Another thing. Inspector Blaine and her captain showed up as I was leaving."

"You make a move?"

"No."

"Good. At least we know she's on the street and with Dresnik around, she'll be easy pickings. Hey, get back to the restaurant. I'm getting ready for the French to show up tonight and I have a job for you."

"What?"

"I need you to go to the DA candidates' debate tonight and keep an eye on things."

Wexler started the car. "Leaving now."

Kayla and Dresnik didn't talk for the remainder of the ride. As she pulled into the Metronome's garage once again, he said, "I have an idea."

"Okay."

"You're not going to like it."

"Tell me anyway." She cruised up the first level.

"Where are you going to stay tonight?"

"Across the bay somewhere."

"What if you stayed in the city? Dangle a bit, see who comes along."

"Not after the safe house, Captain."

"Kayla, it might be the only chance we get to grab somebody. You'll have plenty of protection."

"We told *Margot* she'd have plenty of protection."

"More than what we had at the house. We'll keep the information close like before. Maybe the mole will trip up."

Kayla rounded the second level.

"I don't know."

"Think it over."

Kayla remained quiet as she reached the third level and Dresnik guided her to where he'd parked his car. She stopped behind the blue Ford with city plates.

Kayla stared forward, her face a tight mask of concentration. She could only wonder what her father would think of her situation. If she called him, he'd tell her she never should have become a cop and demand she return to Connecticut. She'd never given up before. She couldn't give up now.

Dresnik opened the door. "I'll be in touch." He put one leg out.

"Captain?"

He turned to her.

"Okay, I'll do it," she said.

Dresnik smiled.

Sam Raven sipped his beer and watched Charlie Kline fidget on the other side of the table.

They occupied a corner booth at a small bar. The bar was the first floor of the Union Hotel. It sat on a corner of an intersection near an off-ramp from the Eastbound 80 Skyway to the Bay Bridge. The cars outside made a tremendous racket the loud jukebox could not mask.

Raven sat with a view of the front door and his back to the wall.

"Tell me what you know," Raven said. "What was in the coroner's report?"

"No way," Kline said. "I'm not saying a word until you tell me more about you."

Raven swallowed some beer, watching Kline over the rim of his glass.

"I appreciate what you've done, but I'm sitting here waiting to get whacked."

"If they wanted you dead, they'd have done it while you were still in a cell."

"And you?"

"If I wanted you dead, why are you here talking?"

"You want to so you can pick my brain before you put a bullet in it."

"Not my style."

"Great to hear. Start talking, *Mister* Raven, or no deal. I'll walk out of here and take my chances."

Raven glanced at the liquid in his glass. The light above the booth reflected in the beer, bringing the sharp amber color alive.

He said, "I was the victim of a crime once. Now I try to help other victims if they're alive. If they're dead, I avenge them."

Kline's face twisted into an expression of disbelief.

"You're insane."

Raven looked up at him. "It's all true."

"What happened?"

"None of your business." He pulled the locket he wore around his neck from under his shirt. "What happened is in here." He jammed the locket into its place.

"You expect me to spill my guts—"

"I expect you, *Charlie*, to help me help you. I've told you all I'm going to say. Now it's your turn."

Kline cursed and swallowed some beer. He took a breath and drank some more. Setting his glass down, he said, "What do you want to know?"

"Tell me about the report you managed to get. What was in it?"

"The real cause of death, for one thing," Kline said. He grabbed his glass with both hands, as if holding on for life. "The coroner found cocaine and alcohol in Whitlow's system. Enough cocaine to kill a horse."

"Forced overdose?"

"Probably."

"Why did the coroner release a report saying heart failure?"

"You don't get it, do you?"

"Explain it to me, Charlie. I'm a slow learner. Explain it to me like I'm a five-year-old."

"I should use small words?"

"Use whichever words you deem appropriate."

"This whole city is corrupt." The reporter leaned forward. "The top people in government, law enforcement, the whole shebang, are on the take. Everybody's doing the bidding of somebody else, who's following the orders of somebody above them."

"How do they get away with this?"

"It's ingrained in the city's DNA, man. From the beginning of its existence."

"The press is no help?"

"The press won't touch it. The press pretends it doesn't exist. You saw what happened to me. We all know if we push too hard, we're going to have an accident, so we go along and we don't question anything.

"All we do," Kline continued, "is regurgitate what the government says. There's never any proper investigation, no hard questions. Whatever they say gets printed or put on TV. It's madness. I didn't get into this business to kneel before the powers that be."

"You want to be Woodward and Bernstein."

"Exactly."

"Instead?"

"I have to do what I'm told or I'm out on my ass. My other option is a rinky-dink newspaper in Idaho, and I don't want to report on new stoplights or the town's new Walmart."

"Newspapers are dying."

"I know."

"How about the web? Put the story up yourself."

"It still puts me in danger. The whole point is to avoid getting killed, right?"

"All right," Raven said. "Why Whitlow?"

"I got sources who tell me things."

"Like what?"

"You mentioned Dixon King. He's the big man in this town. He runs the local mob, answers to the commission in New York City."

"How long has he been here?"

"Couple decades. He's in his 60s now. Mid-30s when he arrived. He was promoted after the other boss had a stroke and died. There was a lot of violence when he showed up. The rest of the crew didn't like somebody from outside taking over, but they were, you know, dealt with. Not always quietly."

Raven nodded. It was a familiar story to him.

Kline said, "A snitch told me King has something going on and needs protection from the top. Dan Whitlow stood in his way. He might have been a hypocrite, but he wasn't going to be bought off."

"Blackmail?"

"So what?" Kline said. "A scandal might force Whitlow out, but King needs to control the replacement."

"I thought so."

Kline took another drink. "I thought I had enough this time, if only I could find somebody to publish it."

"There are two other candidates running for district attorney still."

"Yeah."

"Which one is King's candidate?"

"I have no idea."

"All right, tell me something else. The cops would have raided your apartment after your arrest."

"I know."

"You keep your stuff there?"

Kline nodded. "Yeah."

"What did they get?"

"A statement from my source regarding the hooker who brought Whitlow the coke. Another statement from the prostitute herself."

"Uh-huh. Where's the hooker?"

"I don't know. I referred her to an inspector I know. You'd have to ask her."

"You sent her to the cops?"

"Most of the cops on the SFPD are good people. It's the leadership that's corrupt. If my story got far enough, they'd have a tougher time keeping the truth from coming out. If only it got far enough. That's asking a lot."

"You should have known better. If the hooker has vanished—"

"What else am I supposed to do? I still believe in due process."

"Who's the inspector?"

"Her name's Kayla Blaine."

"Where's your original source, the one who told you about the hooker?"

"A guy in the Tenderloin, he's homeless. His name is Hank. He keeps his ears open for things. He's been a police informant, too."

"Where can I find Hank?"

"Hit any of the bars, he'll be in one, or you'll find him sleeping in an alley. He doesn't like the shelters."

"How do I reach Inspector Blaine?"

Kline took out his cell phone and scrolled through his contact list, reading off Kayla's number. Raven didn't write it down but repeated it twice.

"What about the source who tipped you to the business?

The one who told you what King is doing."

"I can't tell you who my source is."

"You can't afford to keep it quiet, Charlie."

Kline sighed. "He's one of King's lieutenants. A man named Biggins. Tyrone Biggins."

Raven memorized the name, but Kline had no home address. He knew Biggins ran one of King's nightclubs on Essex Street, called Teaser.

"You need to get out of town, Charlie."

"You said so already."

"I wasn't kidding."

"If I run, I'll be arrested again, and looking at serious charges."

"Won't matter. You'll be dead. Once I get this sorted, you'll be clear, and it will be safe to return. Not till then."

"What if you fail?"

"Good luck wherever you end up."

"And never stop looking over my shoulder?"

"Yeah."

Kline's shoulders sank. "Great."

Raven lifted his glass to his mouth. "Finish your beer."

CHAPTER TEN

Charlie Kline gave Raven a quick goodbye and jumped out of the BMW. He didn't look back as he entered the building, took the stairs two at a time, and hurried to his apartment.

The cops had left yellow tape across his door. CRIME SCENE. He ripped down the tape and used his key to get inside.

In his bedroom, he packed a small suitcase, and headed for the door. He paused halfway out.

No.

He wasn't a coward. He wasn't going to run and hide like a frightened cat at the sight of a Rottweiler. He could lay low in the city, keep his ear to the ground, and find a way to assist Raven and especially Kayla Blaine.

He pulled the apartment door shut and left the building.

Raven returned to the Hyatt on the Embarcadero and went for a walk. He crossed Embarcadero to the pier on the other side. The massive Bay Bridge stretched across the bay. Treasure and Yerba Buena Islands marked the halfway point to the other side. Raven watched boats crisscrossing the water. The salty air felt good on his skin.

Around him, people walked or jogged, some of the joggers laboring harder than others. Cars rumbled on the street. A MUNI transit train followed tracks along the center of the street to an underground station. The train seemed like it was melting into the pavement. Clear blue sky, bright sun and a light wind. Not a bad place to spend a few moments to let one clear his head.

Or call for more information.

Raven faced the water again, leaned his elbows on a steel rail, and dialed a number on his cell.

It was an international call, and he'd be waking up his friend and mentor Oscar Morey in Sweden, but Oscar wouldn't mind. He looked after Raven like a father, and Raven appreciated the man's attention. Often, he sorely needed it.

Oscar Morey hadn't always been on the side of the angels. He was an underworld character, well known in Europe, but one who managed never to spend a day in jail. With ears to the ground in many areas, and contacts all over the world, there wasn't anything he didn't know, or could learn, if given enough time.

Years earlier, when a much younger Raven was in Paris to kill a man responsible for several murders, Morey had intercepted him with a warning. Stay out of our business. You don't want this kind of trouble. Raven explained why his target had to die and drew Morey to his side. Some crimes were too heinous for even Morey to tolerate, and he allowed Raven to finish his mission.

When Raven finally confronted the killer, he made him kneel before shooting him in the head.

After Raven saved one of Morey's kids from certain death, the underworld legend pledged his support. From there, the bond between them grew stronger. Raven was smart enough to know when fortune handed him a talisman. In this case, a crusty old bastard named Oscar Morey.

"Should I bother telling you what time it is?" Morey growled after Raven said hello.

"You old folks don't need as much sleep as us young bucks," Raven said.

"What a load of crap. Wait till you're my age, young man, you'll see."

"I should be so lucky."

"Where are you?"

"San Francisco."

"What's cooking?"

"The usual meal. The same sickness I find all over the world, Oscar. It makes a guy wonder why he works so hard."

"If you didn't fight, even a losing battle, you couldn't live with yourself."

"True."

"What do you need?"

"First, a trace on a smart phone. I want to know where it is."

"Is it a woman?"

"How'd you guess?"

"Typical. Hang on."

Raven looked down at the murky water slapping against rocks.

"I'm back," Oscar said. "Go ahead."

Raven repeated Inspector Blaine's number from memory.

"I'll tag it and call you. Might take a while. What's number two?"

"Anything you can find on a local mobster named Tyrone Biggins. He runs a nightclub called Teaser, if it helps."

"You want a home address?"

"Anything."

"Okay."

"What time is it there?" Raven said.

"Almost time for breakfast, if you're an old fart."

Raven laughed. "I missed breakfast today. Have an all-meat omelet in my memory."

"I'll be in touch, Sam. Be reckless."

"Always."

Raven ended the call with a smile.

He checked his watch. Almost time for dinner. He'd get out of his suit, wash the oil out of his hair, and get into normal clothes. The restaurant at the hotel beckoned. After dinner, a nap. He had a long night ahead. He was going into the Tenderloin to look for a man named Hank.

Wexler found King in the kitchen at Martha's tasting a thin slice of medium rare beef. The head chef waited for his reaction.

King chewed, said, "Wow," with his mouth full, and gave the chef a thumbs up. He swallowed. "Yes, more of that."

Wexler waited in the doorway, watching the busy staff at their stations. Each had a part of the meal to prepare. Knives tapped cutting boards. Spoons bumped the sides of pots. Steam and delicious aromas filled the space. Wexler grumbled to himself. He'd have to sit and watch a couple of politicians run their mouths while the boss enjoyed the fine meal.

Oh, well. He had his job to do.

King finally noticed him. When the boss did, he clapped his hands and told the kitchen staff good job and led Wexler to his office.

"Smells great," Wexler said, "whatever it is."

Wexler stood in front of King's desk as the boss slid into his chair. Wexler sat in front of the desk. "I can't pronounce it," the boss continued. "I asked the guys if they knew any French dishes, they said yes, and I told them to get to work. I'll let the head chef announce each one as it's served."

"When do you expect Joulbert and his people?"

"Seven-thirty. The debate starts at 6:30. I can't be in two places at once, obviously."

"I'm supposed to sit there and look mean or something?"

"It's what you do best, Leo." King laughed. "We can't let our friend think we've lost interest."

Wexler nodded.

"When you're done, come back around here, I'm sure there will be leftovers you can take home."

"Sounds fine." Wexler didn't leave the chair.

"Why are you still sitting there?" King asked.

"Remember I saw another guy's name on the bail form? Sam Raven?"

"And?"

Wexler said, "I got to thinking on the drive over. We lose some street guys. This guy Raven comes out of nowhere. I'm thinking there's a connection."

"Think we should inquire?"

"I strongly suggest we find out who he is. He's not a lawyer in San Francisco. He's also not a lawyer anywhere else in the state."

King nodded. "All right. I'll get on it. You get going. Get a front row seat at the debate."

"Where's it at?"

"Top of the Mark. Sky lounge on the 19th floor." King pulled out a desk drawer, removed a small envelope, and passed it to Wexler. "Your invitation. Small audience, all invited guests, and press. Submit a question if you want."

Wexler rose from the chair with a chuckle. "They won't like what I want to ask."

"Here's something else." King removed a manila envelope from the desk drawer. "Talk to you-know-who about the talking points I put down."

Wexler took the second envelope. "Will do. Good luck tonight."

"It will be great," King said as Wexler reached the doorway. "It's the start of a beautiful friendship."

Wexler stood in the hallway a moment to take in the smells from the kitchen one last time. Something was sizzling and it was a soundtrack punctuating scent.

He scoffed. *Leftovers.*

But at least he'd get a taste.

Wexler pushed open the alley door and returned to his car.

CHAPTER ELEVEN

King remained behind his desk, looking at his movie posters for the umpteenth time. He'd spent many a Friday in movie theaters as a teenager, not always paying to get in. Two of the gang would buy tickets, and pop open the outer theater doors for the rest to sneak in. He'd especially loved the horror shows. Some were cheesy enough to be comedies.

His cell phone rang. He picked it up from his desk and recognized the number right away.

"A direct call this time?"

"Have to," a voice said.

"Tell me you know where Inspector Blaine is."

"She's going into protective custody to try and smoke out the mole."

"Will it succeed?" King said.

"You tell me."

King considered his answer, resting his left elbow on the desk and holding the phone to his ear. He tapped the blotter with the index finger of his other hand.

"Who knows about this?"

"Same amount who knew about the safe house. They want to see if they can find out who's telling secrets."

"Does she know anything?"

"She says no. The hit happened before the hooker said much more than her name."

"But she's seen Kline's information."

"I think she only knows what he mentioned to her verbally."

King tapped the blotter some more. His working assumption was Inspector Blaine had seen Kline's information and could testify to what she'd read. If she didn't know anything, good for her. But she remained a threat in another area: she'd survived the hit on the safe house. She could testify to *that* for sure. She still needed to go.

"Listen," King said, "we're going to have to put you at risk. I'm meeting with the Frenchmen tonight. We're moving ahead and there can't be any risk. She survived the safe house; she could still hurt us."

The caller didn't respond.

"But maybe there's a way to mitigate the damage," King continued. "Can you put some of our people on the watch?"

"Sure."

"We can set up a fall guy. That will be your mole. Case closed, Blaine's out of the way, nothing to stop us."

"I know exactly who to call."

"Be careful, Dresnik. I need you."

Captain Marty Dresnik let out a laugh over the line. "We need each other, Mr. King."

The sky lounge at the Intercontinental Mark Hopkins Hotel on Nob Hill was a lousy place for a debate.

The hotel counted among its claims to fame the business of celebrities, presidents, and global dignitaries. The lounge sat on the 19th floor and offered a terrific view.

Leonard Wexler followed a group to the entrance where

they showed their invitations. Wexler found a seat up front. A small sign written in calligraphy said the bar was closed. *How fancy*, Wexler decided. He supposed the last thing two politicians needed were liquored up audience members shouting uncomfortable questions. It would have been hilarious to watch.

The panoramic windows offered a view of the city skyline Wexler barely acknowledged. Only the tourists cared, and the lounge had been built with only tourists in mind. Wexler had to admit it was hard to not look, even though San Francisco no longer impressed him. It wasn't New York City.

The roofs of a bunch of buildings and the shimmering bay beyond mattered little. The water looked nice at high altitude.

The regular tables and chairs had been replaced with two rows of chairs. The tables faced the window to the left as Wexler entered, where a table and seats for the candidates waited. A pull-down shade covered the window behind the table. Podium to one side, signs at each seat identifying which candidate occupied the chair. Speakers in three corners throughout the lounge.

News reporters and camera operators mixed with the growing number of invited guests. The cameras were set up in the rear, the reporters crowding up front. A sound engineer fussed with the microphones on the candidates' table.

He wished the bar were open. There should have been snacks served. Wexler hoped nobody heard his stomach rumble. He had visions of *leftovers* in his head.

The chatter in the room grew in volume. Wexler tuned out the sound, sat with crossed legs and arms, and stared ahead. The font on the skirt read *The Candidates Debate!* and showed the date and time.

He wondered how much time the pair would waste talking about Whitlow. This was the first debate since the man's death.

It was supposed to have happened sooner, but the incumbent had to drop dead.

Presently the moderator for the night stepped behind the podium and called for everybody to take their seats. Wexler shrugged. He was already seated. He could ignore the lady.

The moderator announced she was Jackie Sandmore, the editor-in-chief of the *Chronicle*. She said, "That's Jackie as in Gleason, and sand as in you want more sand at the beach!"

Polite laughter. Wexler shook his head. Idiot. Who liked sand? He hated sand. It was coarse and got everywhere and into everything. And it wasn't like the entire event was being shown on television. The news people were there to ask questions and record enough to get sound bites for eleven o'clock. Nobody cared about the fat moderator.

Jackie Sandmore—"sand" as in fuck you and your beach—wore a cheap blue suit. Her blouse struggled against her bulk. Short curly hair, puffy face. She had to be near 60. An inch-thick layer of makeup did nothing to smooth her appearance.

"I want to welcome you to tonight's debate," she said, "featuring Supervisor Chelsea Brandt, and attorney Stephen Kennedy. Let's welcome Supervisor Brandt first. We do ladies first around here!"

Forced laugh. Right on cue. Courtesy laughs behind him. Wexler wanted to make a list of anybody who thought the line was funny and pitch them off the roof.

Jackie Sandmore—sand as in get this shit out of my crotch—turned to her right. She greeted Chelsea Brandt with a formal handshake and showed her to the table. Brandt sat on the left side.

Wexler smiled as Brandt collected herself and placed her hands, folded, in front of her on the tabletop. She was the opposite of Jackie Sandmore, mid-40s, yet looking younger. Long blonde hair, blue eyes, and a decent figure—all the things the cameras loved.

"And Mr. Stephen Kennedy, Esquire," Jackie Sandmore continued.

Stephen Kennedy shook the moderator's hand and took the remaining seat. He wasn't related to the *Kennedy* Kennedys, but and had been mistaken for being so. Trim, good-looking, short black hair and bright eyes—the camera loved him, too. Wexler recalled a crack made by the wife of Tyrone Biggins, one of King's lieutenants: "He can press my charges any time!"

Wexler hated that line too.

Cameras flashed. Jackie Sandmore—sand as in goddammit I'm still shaking this shit out of the cooler—picked up a pile of index cards. She announced this-or-that homeless advocacy group, and some mothers against guns group, sponsored the event. Whatever Jackie Sandmore said, Wexler didn't care. His eyes were on King's choice for district attorney. He couldn't help but smile when he and the candidate made eye contact.

CHAPTER TWELVE

Chelsea Brandt's eyes twinkled as she offered Wexler a smile.

Bought and paid for and ready to take over.

Wexler's eyes landed on Kennedy, the upright choirboy, the boy scout, the man who couldn't be touched. But like Whitlow, he had a weakness for women not his wife. Wexler, who'd never had much luck with women, had no trouble busting a punk's kneecaps or shooting cops. But talking to a woman? Nuts. He didn't know what went through other guys' heads when they did stupid things to screw up their relationships. Kennedy was a guy who could screw up what he had but had so far pulled the wool over his wife's eyes. His wife either wasn't suspicious enough or didn't care. Maybe there was more to their relationship than Wexler realized. Was Kennedy's philandering a symptom of a larger problem?

Why was he giving the man the benefit of the doubt? He shook his head. Make a guy sit alone for five minutes and his mind starts wandering. He had a job to do. *Focus.*

Dixon King hadn't yet exploited Kennedy's weakness because Whitlow needed to be taken out first.

Poor dumb bastard. You're next. Say goodbye to all of this.

Jackie Sandmore opened with a moment of silence for Dan Whitlow. She noted the debate had to be postponed because of his death, and they would carry on in the interest of the people, democracy, law and order, and all the happy horseshit Whitlow stood for.

Wexler had no problem keeping silent, but had a little trouble stifling a chuckle.

And then the debate began.

"Our first question is from Mr. Emmett Chandler of San Francisco." She smiled into the audience but probably had no idea who Emmett Chandler was. "The question is for Mr. Kennedy. San Francisco's homeless problem remains out of control despite city health care, food programs, and shelters. Crimes committed by homeless continue to plague San Franciscans and push away needed tourist dollars. As district attorney, what will your position be on homeless crime?"

Stephen Kennedy cleared his throat and straightened in the chair. "Tough question," he said, pulling his microphone a little closer. "It's not so easy as to say we can cure homelessness like it's a *disease*. We're dealing with people who, in some cases, aren't capable of functioning in society, either because of drug addiction or mental illness. Instead of trying to cure something we don't need to cure, I'm interested in finding ways of helping those unable to help themselves. Let's give them the best care possible, let them know they're loved and wanted in whichever shape or form they come to us in. Let's keep San Francisco a beacon of hope for those who don't have any.

"And to answer your question specifically, Mr. Chandler," Kennedy continued, "if a homeless person commits a crime, it's out of desperation. I would revisit my opening statement and urge the city to do more along those lines, which will keep homeless out of the justice system. If you have a full belly and the care you need, there's no need to commit a crime."

WICKED CITY | 99

Scattered applause.

"Mrs. Brandt, your response."

Wexler grinned and waited for Brandt to prove she was such a bigger bleeding heart. Maybe she'd rip open her blouse and show her actual ticker bleeding through the center of her chest.

"Mr. Kennedy has the right idea, but the wrong approach," Brandt said. "I'm not going to address the question of care. It isn't the job of the district attorney to comment on the city's homeless policy. The district attorney's job is to speak for the people and prosecute crime. If a homeless person is trying to purposefully be thrown in jail as a way out, we need to do more. I'm all for increasing care. We indeed need to *increase* care for those who require attention, but we have to think of citizens who are *paying* for the care of others. We need to make sure they are protected from random acts of violence while out walking their dog. While I'm happy to continue working with the city supervisors on this issue, and the record reflects my passion for the homeless, I promise crimes will be prosecuted with as much vigor as the law requires."

No applause.

If Brandt caught Wexler's frown, she betrayed no evidence.

Other questions followed a similar bent. What do we do about gun crime? Will you prosecute police who break the law? Will you be lenient on minor drug offenders since pot is mostly legal now? On and on for three hours before a tired-looking Jackie Sandmore—sand as in I've had enough let's go home, I can't get this crap out of my toes—asked the candidates for a closing statement.

They both chose to use their time to honor the late Dan Whitlow, promising to keep his spirit alive, since his spirit was the spirit of San Francisco, and on and on. Wexler only thought about whether there were any leftovers still at the restaurant.

The debate over, the candidates spent another hour on

follow-up questions from the press. Wexler managed to shake Chelsea Brandt's hand and tell her she did well.

"Thank you."

"I'll make sure to update our mutual friend."

Through a big smile she said, "I'm looking forward to our next meeting."

Wexler leaned close, Brandt brushing away her nearby assistant. He said, "I need to see you."

"Black Lincoln in the garage," she said.

He nodded.

Wexler slipped away, passing Kennedy, who was holding up a finger to pause a reporter while he answered an urgent cell phone call. He advised he only had another five minutes before he needed to depart. His younger assistant helped escort him through the crowd once those five minutes had passed. Wexler watched them head for the elevator.

Wexler took the stairs and enjoyed the solitude as he descended.

The exercise helped him work up an appetite. He hoped his follow-up chat with Chelsea Brandt didn't take too long. He hoped traffic on the way to Martha's Restaurant wasn't too heavy.

Stephen Kennedy shook off his assistant and drove home in his own car. He drove a little faster than he should have, but he needed to get home *fast*. He had a guest waiting.

Her name was Melissa Doyle, brunette, rockin' body, and a knockout overall.

As his "campaign advisor", she actually fulfilled the role well and had plenty of experience. She also had experience raising polls—to whit, Kennedy's dick. With his wife out of town on business for another few days, Kennedy and

Melissa had taken advantage of the extra "campaign prep" to improve his poll performance as often as time allowed and even when it didn't because nobody did nothing until Stephen Kennedy, candidate for district attorney, actually showed up to do something.

She'd called to tell him she was waiting at the condo in next to nothing, so he'd better get there fast before she found another stud.

He reached the underground garage of his building and cursed the security gate for taking so long to raise.

Parked the car.

Hopped in the elevator.

Six floors up.

Steady, man, steady. Show some dignity. Shoulders back. Smile. It was a good night.

He advanced down the hallway and unlocked his condo and stepped into the dark entry way.

"Uh-oh," he called out, dropping wallet, keys and cell phone on a table near the door. "It's dark and I'm scared."

A woman's voice called out, "Follow the sound of my voice."

"What if I need more than that?"

Melissa Doyle let out a seductive moan with enough erotic promise to melt any man.

"That's more like it."

Kennedy shed his suit jacket, tossing it on the floor of his bedroom. The shapely Melissa Doyle lay on the bed. The glow from the nightstand alarm clock showed indeed what next to nothing she was wearing. The see-through nightie barely covered her hips.

"Hurry up," she said, rolling onto her side and running a hand along her smooth hip. "I've been waiting. And *waiting.*" Another moan. "You don't want to know what I had to do while I was waiting, Stephen, honey."

Kennedy yanked off his tie and started unbuttoning his shirt, one button at a time, not fast enough, and who was the idiot who made shirt buttons so freaking hard to undo when a guy was about to get laid? He could have given the shirt a good pull and risk losing some buttons, but it was a custom-made Armani, and not even Melissa Doyle's sinful delights were worth losing buttons on a custom-made Armani. "Tell me."

"The battery in my poor pocket rocket died!"

He laughed and shrugged off the shirt and straddled her with his knees on either side of her hips, and dived between her breasts, where she was sensitive, and she laughed as his kisses tickled her, wrapping her arms around his head, pulling him closer, wrapping her legs around him next to lock him in place. He entered her fiercely and she urged him on. There was nothing tender about their encounters, simply pure animal lust between them. His wife was boring. Melissa Doyle wasn't boring. And when the see-through nightie finally landed on the floor with the rest of his clothes, she showed him once again how un-boring she could be.

Wexler waited in the garage beneath the Mark Hopkins, standing against a pillar near parked cars. He watched Chelsea Brandt's black Lincoln Continental across the aisle. The garage's drab concrete amplified the outside chill. Other guests came and went. No second looks at him.

Chelsea finally arrived, her advisor in tow, going over the debate, talking about the next day's agenda. The chat took forever. Wexler shifted his feet to stay comfortable, but a guy can only stand for so long before his lower back started getting sore. With the bulk he carried, Wexler's back bothered him a lot after a long day.

Finally, she was alone. The advisor drove off in her own car.

Wexler stepped around the pillar and crossed the aisle.

"Finally," Chelsea said. She climbed into the Lincoln. Wexler joined her in the passenger seat and removed Dixon King's manila envelope from his jacket pocket.

"Couple things to talk about," he said.

"How's Dixon?"

"Fine."

"The project?"

"Under way as we speak."

"Good."

Wexler scanned the bullet points. "Polls are neck and neck with you two post-Whitlow."

Chelsea Brandt scoffed. "Tell me about it."

"It's time to cut down Mr. Kennedy."

"How?"

"He shares Whitlow's, um—"

"He screws around on his wife."

"Sure."

"All right, so we catch him in the act," she said. "Any ideas?"

Wexler consulted the King's notes. The boss had laid out all the details. "We have one." He told her the plan, providing a phone number to call. The phone number featured a Nevada area code.

"Who is this woman?" Chelsea said.

"Danielle Rawlings. Expensive hooker. She's done a few favors for us, but always through a middle-man."

"I'm the middle-*woman*, is that it?"

"Exactly."

"Sounds fine," she said. "But if this goes south, she'll know my name."

"It won't go south."

"It's not your backside if it does."

"Do what you're told. Let us watch your backside."

She stared at him.

"One way or another," Wexler said, "we're going to weaken Kennedy's campaign, and make sure you win the election. It will be clean. We can't afford accusations of fraud. We get pictures of him with this woman, and he'll do whatever we tell him to. He'll be glad to assist if it means avoiding a scandal."

"Fine," she said.

He put the paper down and looked at her. With her long blonde hair cascading down her shoulders, her left elbow propped on the door to support her head, she looked attractive. She had her own family at home. The wedding ring on her left hand sparkled. Wexler had nobody. He'd go home to an empty condo and drink a beer while staring out the window at the lighted city and curse his life and go to bed. He pressed his lips together to find a way to end the conversation.

"Anything else?" she finally said.

"Keep doing what you're doing, and we'll keep up our end."

"Of course."

Wexler said goodnight and pushed open the passenger door. He returned to his car and tried not to think about his racing pulse. He wanted to think about *leftovers* instead. Those he could handle.

CHAPTER THIRTEEN

Dinner started perfectly.

Seated at the head of the table in Martha's banquet room, Dixon King, in the sharpest suit he owned, introduced his side. Abelard Joulbert introduced his people. Each faction sat on one side of the table, Joulbert to King's right, and the lieutenants smiled and greeted each other. The conversation flowed as the restaurant crew brought out each course of the meal.

King had insisted, upon arrival, Joulbert and his three companions relax in their hotel, get over jet lag, walk around the city a little, and let the salty bay air clear their heads after flying in from the other side of the world. It was an agreeable arrangement. King only regretted he hadn't been able to solve all of their problems before the meeting took place.

Abelard Joulbert cut an impressive figure. He wore a white suit, his well-tanned face paramount, full head of dark hair. He was shorter and slighter than King but carried himself as if he were as big as Wexler. King saw determination in his eyes, an important feature. He knew Joulbert was facing a hard time at home with the government crackdown. If he didn't turn things around with the Pacific Alliance, as they were calling it, he was a dead man. King was a dead man too if it didn't work. They both had plenty of reason to stay the course and make it happen.

After dessert, the staff served coffee, and the conversation finally turned to business.

"It's funny," King began, stirring cream into his coffee. "When I grew up in New York, we were poor, man, I mean we had *nothing*. My old man worked two jobs. My mother took care of me and my brother and when Dad got home at night, she worked late at a hospital cleaning the toilets. I'd sit by our living room window and look out at the street. I'd see all the nice cars. The local wise guys were always wandering around, and boy did they look sharp."

Joulbert listened, nodding.

"I wanted to be one of those guys, right?" King said. "Those guys didn't have to worry about paying the rent because they had hundred-dollar bills sticking out of their pockets. That's what it's all about, right? Not having to worry about things."

Joulbert sipped his coffee and nodded again.

"It took a long time," King concluded, "but I got there."

"We have our own worries," the Frenchman said, his English terrific, accent light, "but, yes. I understand."

King made a dismissive gesture. "We only worry when the sons of bitches we pay to look the other way and take care of things don't do their jobs."

Joulbert shrugged. "Our good fortune can turn on one election, my friend. You haven't seen it yet. It happened to us in Paris. The conservatives swept the election. Now they're making it tough to do business."

"Oh, I get it. I'm working hard to make sure the election we're concerned with now goes our way."

He outlined the Whitlow situation in detail, and how his people engineered the desired result.

"Impressive," Joulbert said.

King left out any mention of on-going problems. There was no sense worrying Joulbert. He didn't want the Frenchman experiencing a sudden lack of confidence.

He fully expected the final problem, Inspector Kayla Blaine, to be history by sunrise.

"But why the district attorney's office?" Joulbert said. "Why is the position so important to you?"

King sniffed. It was a fair question. He said, "The DA controls what cases get prosecuted and which ones do not. With a DA in our pocket, we can make sure any case related to us doesn't go forward. And, as a bonus, the DA can put attorneys in place who are easy to control too. His or her own people, people she can trust to follow orders and keep their mouths shut. It's a security blanket. We get tremendous dividends."

Joulbert nodded.

"There will be, of course, sacrifices," King said. "Sometimes a case needs to go forward. We can arrange those. Give the cops on the front line enough to satisfy them, keep them at bay, but our main concerns are always protected."

"I understand."

"Our arrangement is going to work," King said. He sipped his coffee. Perfect temperature. He swallowed some more. "But to your other point, yes, we'll have this issue again in the future. By then we'll be so locked in no law-and-order punk is going to ruin it."

"We have questions," Joulbert said.

"I have answers," King said. He smiled.

"The areas of the Pacific Coast where you have no influence. What are your plans?"

"I got a stockpile of guns in a few warehouses. When the time comes, I also got a list of people we will hire to do some rough stuff if the other syndicates won't play ball. We have enough ordnance to blow them into orbit."

The conversation carried on into the night. Questions about how King would receive product from France. How he would distribute said product and funnel money back to France. Joulbert seemed satisfied with the answers King supplied.

Wexler finally showed up. King had one of the wait staff take him into the kitchen for the plate of food King had promised.

Kayla Blaine had no idea how long she was supposed to wait.

She sat with two other cops in a small room at the Union Hotel, and the walls didn't keep out the street noise at all. From the window, she could watch the cars back up on the off-ramp prior to surging onto city streets.

Across the table, hair tied in a ponytail and shoulder holster in place, was her friend, Sergeant Lori Morgan. She had requested to work the protection detail. Kayla didn't want her there in case the worst happened. But she was also glad Lori was there. The positive/negative thoughts made Kayla feel strange. Part of her was relieved to have a friend. Part of her was afraid for her friend. But she appreciated Lori wanting to be there because.

The other cop in the room, somebody pulled onto the detail from traffic, whom Kayla had not met before, sat in a corner across the room, reading a fishing magazine. He too wore the prerequisite shoulder harness and service automatic. But he also had a Remington 870 pump shotgun propped next to the chair.

Kayla had questioned the use of an officer from the traffic division. Dresnik said Officer Peter York had worked VIP protection in Afghanistan while in the Marines, and he knew the drill. Kayla had wanted to argue they weren't supposed to use people not involved with the original safe house operation, but realized she was the only survivor of said operation, so the net needed to be a little wider this time. The goal was to smoke out the mole. She accepted his answer. As she was an officer who didn't fit the requirements of a high-risk witness, she didn't get the advantage of SWAT.

Two other officers sat in a car on the street, parked in front of the hotel, part of a rotating crew who would change every eight hours.

Dresnik had headquarters covered.

As more time ticked by, Kayla began to wonder if she was a target, or if she was overreacting.

A nagging yet unformed thought suggested otherwise. She'd always listened to her sixth sense and wasn't about to reject it now.

After not finding reporter Charlie Kline at the county jail, she and Dresnik put in a request to see the evidence collected from his apartment. But since Kline was arrested in another area of the city, with another division responsible for his case, the request had to go through channels. Dresnik would need to explain why he wanted to see the evidence. Red tape. Always red tape.

In the meantime, Kayla Blaine sat, waited, and grew more irritated.

The walls shook as cars rumbled along the off-ramp.

"This place sucks," she said.

Lori laughed. "You should see some of the places I spend my nights at. This is way nicer."

Officer Peter York looked up from his magazine long enough to smile and returned to his reading.

She and Lori played gin. Endless games of gin. The slap of cards on the table couldn't compete with the car sounds.

"No wonder this place is so run down," Kayla said. "Nobody wants to stay here with these godawful cars running by."

"I think the owner," Lori said, "also runs the bar downstairs."

"Must be nice to tell the drunks unable to drive home they can crash upstairs."

"For a price."

Kayla laughed. "Sure."

The old wallpaper had taken on a greenish shade Kayla didn't want to know about. The carpet was clean, but there were patches of worn-in dirt only a serious scrubbing would remove. The mattress rested on a metal frame dotted with patina. The place was old. There might have been some charm in the age if the presentation was better. It had no charm at all.

"Gin!" Lori called, slapping down her winning hand. Kayla tossed her cards on the table, stood up, and bent over to touch her toes. She sat down again.

"Remind me why I joined the cops?" she said.

"The glamour," Lori said. "It's like TV, remember?"

Kayla sighed.

Officer Peter York's cell phone rang. He set his fishing magazine on the floor and answered with, "Hey, babe."

Lori gathered the cards on the table and began shuffling the deck.

"I think I'm finished, Lori."

"One more hand."

Kayla said all right. "Then maybe we can find something on TV."

"Without cable?"

The hotel only had local channels accessed by antennas on the roof.

"Keeps getting better," Kayla said.

Officer Peter York mumbled through his conversation. Kayla and Lori ignored him as Lori dealt cards.

Officer Peter York ended his call and stood to stretch.

A lull in vehicle traffic allowed silence to settle a moment.

Commotion outside. Yelling. Glass breaking.

Lori began to rise from her chair.

Kayla said, "What's happening?"

The gunshot cracked in the room, Kayla reacting with a shout, but not from being startled. Blood from Lori's head wound reached from her from the other side of the table. Lori, half out of the chair, dropped back onto the cushion, her body tipping slowly to bump into the wall.

Kayla dove for the ground as Peter York's second shot tore a hole in her chair. Kayla's elbows burned as they dug into the carpet, and she grabbed the SIG Sauer P229 from her shoulder harness. As York moved around the bed to stand over her and deliver his next shot, she fired. Two rounds through his groin captured his attention, his squeal filling the room. She fired twice more, the .40 caliber rounds punching neat holes through his neck and face to decorate the greenish wallpaper with splashes of red.

Kayla jumped onto the bed, reaching the other side before Peter York's body hit the floor. She flung open the door and charged down the narrow hallway.

Two figures emerged from the stairway at the end of the hall, both males, thin, dark-skinned. They aimed guns at her. She dove forward again as slugs flashed over her body. She rolled left, bumping into the wall, settling the SIG's sights on one killer. There was no way she could fire fast enough to get them both. She'd take one with her. It was the only consolation she could find.

Two shots, two more, both loud booms bouncing between the hallway walls. The killers collapsed on top of each other.

Kayla steadied her aim on the third figure who appeared from the stairway.

"Inspector Blaine!"

"Hold it right there!"

The man raised his hands. In his right, he held a black pistol, an unmistakable .45 automatic.

"Don't you move!"

"Inspector Blaine, we need to go now."

"You twitch and I'll kill you!"

"Your men downstairs are dead! You've been sold out. Come with me now!"

"Give me one reason why I should!"

"Charlie Kline! I bailed him out of jail today and he gave me your name."

The SIG didn't waver in Kayla grip. "Tell me your name."

"Sam Raven."

She blinked. Before her was no lawyer. He wore all black and looked trim and muscular enough to smack down any perp who tried to do something stupid.

But she recognized the name. If nothing else, she needed to find out why he was mixed up in this mess.

"Lower your gun and come with me," Sam Raven said.

"Fine!" She rose from the floor and holstered her gun. Raven put his gun under his jacket.

"Wait," she said.

"Inspector!"

She ran back into the room, grabbed her purse a tote bag, gave poor Lori once last glance, and ran into the hallway where Sam Raven intercepted her. They hustled toward the stairs, stepping over the dead bodies of the two killers.

"You go first," she told him.

Sam Raven didn't argue. He led her down the stairway to the street, the exit depositing them on the sidewalk. She gasped at the sight of the two officers in the unmarked car at the curb. And the two gunmen on the sidewalk, both still clutching smoking submachine guns fitted with suppressors.

"Whoever wanted you dead went to a lot of trouble," Sam

Raven said. "This way."

He didn't try to grab her arm, which she appreciated. She followed him, her senses on autopilot. What was going on? Why was she following this man without question? He might be leading her into a trap. But the dead gunmen on the sidewalk, at the top of the stairs, and the bullets she'd put into Peter York, suggested her idea of a trap wasn't correct. There'd been more firepower sent to kill her than she'd seen in all her years on the force.

Presently they jumped into a BMW 530i Sam Raven had left in an alley. The engine rumbled to life and he stepped on the throttle. The car powered through the alley to the street ahead, where Sam Raven made a sharp right turn into the flow of traffic.

"You are *not* a cop," she said. She jammed her tote and purse in the foot well.

Sam Raven laughed. "Hardly. The last thing you need is a cop."

"The last thing I need is a stranger I know nothing about." She took out her gun and jammed it into his side.

"Hey!"

"Don't *hey* me," she said. "My friend back there is dead, more of my friends died the other night, and I'm next on the list. Don't hey me anything."

"I'm not here to hurt you," Sam Raven said. "I'm trying to solve the problem same as you."

"I don't believe you."

"Believe this. Dixon King started this whole mess by murdering Dan Whitlow." Raven told her what he'd learned from Charlie Kline, about his activity in the city, ending with his ultimate goal. "I'm here to smash this alliance and put King and Joulbert in the grave. You can help me, or I can drop you on the street to fend for yourself."

She withdrew the SIG Sauer but didn't holster the gun. She held it on her lap with her finger alongside the trigger guard.

"Thank you for removing the artillery," Sam Raven said.

"This is crazy."

"I get that a lot," he said.

"Who are you?"

"Sam Raven."

"You *know* what I mean!"

"It's complicated," he said. "I used to be a couple of things. Now, I travel the world, meet exciting people, and usually kill them."

"You're a murderer?"

"I consider myself an instrument of justice," Sam Raven said.

"Responsible to whom?"

He laughed without humor. Sadness flashed through his face. The change in expression startled her.

"We don't have enough time for me to tell you my life story," he said.

"And you're here to kill Dixon King and this Frenchman I've never heard of?"

"Oh, you'll get to know him well, I'm sure," Sam Raven said. "He's going to be a major player in this drama of ours."

Traffic congestion slowed them, but it was a typical night in San Francisco. People living their own lives having no idea what else was going on, or whose life might be turning upside down, or whose life may have ended.

She looked at Sam Raven as he drove. She was both fascinated and confused by him, but maybe he could do what the SFPD hadn't been able to do. One, keep her alive. Two, solve the crime surrounding Dan Whitlow's murder.

If he knew more than she did, and it sounded as if he'd been busy since his arrival, he'd at least identified two major targets.

He wanted King and Joulbert dead. Well, so did she. And he'd have to get in line once she reached them. Sam Raven could get the sloppy seconds. The kills would be hers. No arrests. No red tape. She had friends to avenge. Too many.

Kayla settled into the seat.

Sam Raven drove on.

CHAPTER FOURTEEN

Raven's search for the mysterious Hank in the Tenderloin had gone bust after a few hours; when Oscar Morey called, Raven was glad for the interruption.

"Got a ping on the phone."

"Where?"

"Union Hotel—"

"I know where it is. I was there the other day."

"You heading that way?"

"Right now, as a matter of fact. I've been chasing another lead but it's not panning out."

"Good luck."

"What about Tyrone Biggins?"

"He runs a nightclub called Tease."

"I *know*, Oscar."

"Still looking."

"Hurry."

"Going as fast as I can," Oscar Morey said.

He'd arrived to see the gunmen on the sidewalk shooting into the parked police car, and two more gunners running up the stairs via the sidewalk exit door. He'd charged after them.

As he drove, Kayla said nothing more. He didn't press her.

There was no need to talk for now. She needed to settle down and think of her next moves, and he needed to figure out what to do with her once they returned to the Hyatt. The heat was rising, and he wasn't sure how well he could protect her so close to the flames. Sending her out of harm's way across the bay might be a good idea, but he had a feeling Kayla Blaine wasn't going to agree.

Her friends had been killed. Justice had to be served, steaming hot, without delay. She'd want to stay and fight.

Raven knew those feelings all too well.

They shaped each moment of his life.

Raven parked the BMW in the Hyatt's garage and shut off the motor.

"You're staying here?" she said. Her eyes darted around the interior of the parking structure, already looking for threats.

"It's not a dump. Nobody's going to hurt you here."

"Because I have a big strong protector now?"

"Not what I meant."

"I know what you meant, *Mister* Raven."

"Call me Sam."

Inspector Kayla Blaine shut her eyes and rubbed her face with both hands. Raven noticed the unattended SIG pistol before she did and she grabbed it, her eyes wide as she looked at him, a frightened cat forced into a corner. The gun represented her claws.

Raven only sat and watched her, with his left hand draped over the top of the steering wheel and the other hand resting on the center console.

"I don't want your gun," he said. "I have my own."

"I saw. You're one of those guys who insists on an old .45 pistol?"

"It's not old."

"The design is old."

"Doesn't mean it is less effective than what you have in your hand right now."

She scoffed. "Now you want us to go up to your room like a normal couple?"

"To start. Then you're going to your room."

A frown. "You got me a room?"

"On a hunch at dinner tonight. I thought I'd better have one when we finally connected. I doubted you'd want to sleep in the same room with me. I'd have asked for a roll-out cot, of course."

"And it's the adjoining room, right?"

"No," he said. "I asked, but it's reserved. You're across from me."

"Of course," she said. "Such a gentleman."

"I'm not your enemy, Kayla."

She flinched at the use of her first name. Raven needed to find a way to break down her barriers and fast.

"Thanks," she said, "I seem to have nothing but enemies right now. I'm so *glad* my best friend is a *stranger* who admits *murdering* people all over the world."

Raven kept his voice low and even. "I've never killed anybody the world is going to miss, Kayla. Let's go."

He exited the car first. She followed, purse and tote in hand, so he could lock the car with the key remote. The car chirped and the lights flashed. They stepped into an elevator and rode up in silence.

When Raven pushed open the door of his hotel room, she went in first. Hopefully, her ice wall showed signs of thawing. He shut the door and snapped both locks.

She shut the door to the bathroom and remained inside a few minutes. Raven tossed his jacket on the bed, pulled off the shoulder holster, and threw the harness on top of his jacket. From the room's small refrigerator, which he had filled previously, he selected two cans of 7UP. They didn't need caffeine right now and she certainly wouldn't have accepted booze.

The toilet flushed, the water ran in the sink, and she emerged from the bathroom. She'd wiped the sweat from her face and looked tired.

He handed her a 7UP and she popped the top. She didn't say thank you.

"Pulling me from the scene of the shooting is a mistake," she said.

"We can't go back there now."

"I'm a cop. I can do whatever I want. They know me."

"That's the problem, Kayla."

Another flinch. She didn't want the familiarity. Raven watched her. She crossed the room to plop down at the table. Kayla took a long drink from the soda and set the can on the table. She folded her arms.

"If there's anything you need, we have shops at the hotel and in the complex next door," he said. "Give me your sizes and whatever else you want, and I'll get you what you need."

"You aren't buying me any clothes or anything else. I have enough for a couple of days."

"Also, you shouldn't be out alone at all. We go together or you stay here."

"You have all the answers, don't you?"

"No." Raven sat on the edge of the bed to face her. "All I know I got from Charlie Kline. He explained to me how the city works, the corruption from the top."

"I'm familiar."

"Did he show you any of the statements he took from his sources?"

"Wouldn't have mattered," she said. "We needed the

witness herself."

"Did you read their statements?"

She shook her head. "I didn't want to look at them. He told me the general idea. After that I knew we needed to do the interviews ourselves, so it was official."

"But he told you about the hooker."

"Her name was Margot," Kayla said.

"I didn't know."

"I bet you also didn't know we had her at a police safe house in Colma, and a group of gunmen, like tonight, showed up to kill us all?"

"Hasn't been on the news."

"It wouldn't be," she said. "You can bet people know it happened, but the story's been shit-canned. I have no idea how the department is going to explain a bunch of dead SWAT cops. It's not like they didn't have families or anything."

Raven nodded. "Apart from Kline, all I can offer is my speculation, which I've given you. Based on experience—"

"It's probably correct," she said. "More than likely correct, actually. It makes a lot of sense."

"Has there been any talk of the French coming on?"

"You'd have to ask narcotics. I only show up when somebody's dead."

"Right. But no gossip?"

"I don't know anybody in narcotics," Kayla said. "I used to know somebody in vice. She was killed tonight, right in front of me."

"I'm sorry."

"Sure."

"Kline talked about a source named Hank. A homeless man. I tried to find him in the Tenderloin tonight, but no sale."

"Never heard of him."

"Maybe we can try again tomorrow night."

"You keep using *we* a lot."

Raven took a deep breath. He needed patience. Kayla Blaine needed time. She'd been through hell the last few days. He didn't blame her, but he also needed her to get with the program. Right now, she was her own worst enemy.

CHAPTER FIFTEEN

Kayla said, "I need to call my captain."

"Absolutely not."

"He needs to know where I am."

"Does he? Seems he's known your location a couple of times, and each time somebody has shown up to kill you."

"There's a mole," she said. "Somebody in the department is working with the bad guys. Captain Dresnik is trying to find the mole, not kill me."

"Are you sure?" Raven said. He drank some soda while she gave him a look of disbelief.

"I've been around long enough," he told her, "to know a traitor is usually so close to home they aren't noticed."

"Captain Dresnik is a good man. He wouldn't set us up."

"We can't trust your captain right now, Kayla."

"Stop using my name. I'm Inspector Blaine to you."

"Who else knows about your operation? Who knew about the safe house? Who else knew where you were tonight?"

The color drained from her face.

"I know it's not—"

She cut him off. "Stop! Stop talking!"

Raven went silent. She stood up and paced a moment and

sat down again. Her hands shook. She rested her elbows on her knees and covered her face.

No!

Kayla felt her pulse beating rapidly. Could the person who betrayed her be the captain who had taken her under his wing?

Sam Raven was wrong. He had to be. Dresnik was a good cop. There had never been any sign of corruption from him, not even a fixed ticket. One thing she knew, she couldn't trust him. Not yet. He had a lot to prove.

What she needed to do was get away and hide until the department solved the problems.

She lowered her hands and looked at Sam Raven. The idiot sat on the edge of the bed watching her like she was in a cage. Maybe she was. A cage of paranoia and uncertainty. It wasn't a good place to be.

He started talking again.

"If you stay out of sight," Raven said, **"we probably have** 24 hours before they begin searching for you in earnest."

"The bad guys?"

"The cops. They'll talk to your friends, relatives, the works."

"We have to keep my family out of this."

"Yes. We don't want anybody involved who doesn't need to be."

She finally drank more of her soda, tipping her head to drain the can. She set it down again. "Thanks for the drink."

"Sorry it wasn't stronger."

She forced a laugh. "I wouldn't want your alcohol anyway."

"What you need is sleep."

She nodded.

Raven took out his wallet and removed two key cards. She watched him approach. He set the key cards on the table and returned to the dresser.

"I don't trust you," she said.

"You shouldn't trust anybody."

"You're not going to try and convince me?"

"If what I've done and said so far hasn't helped my case, nothing else I do will convince you. Except time."

"I don't have time."

"It's my job to get you as much time as you should naturally be allowed."

"What's around your neck?"

Raven pulled out the locket from under his shirt and held it up so she could see.

"It's the reason," he said, "I do the things I do."

"Let me see what's inside."

"No."

She waited.

Raven put the locket back down his shirt.

"You don't have to trust me," he said, "but recognize I haven't tried to kill you."

"Yet."

"Right. This is an elaborate ruse to find out what you know before I kill you. Kayla, if I wanted you dead, I certainly would not have taken the risk to bring you here. Those gunmen don't care what you truly know. They only want to keep you from talking about what they think you know."

"You have all the answers."

"I wish," Raven said.

She dropped her eyes to the carpet.

"What you need right now is rest," he repeated. "And a good breakfast tomorrow morning."

She didn't reply. She put her feet on the floor and stood,

scooping up the hotel room key cards while holding her purse and tote bag under her left arm. She walked past him and out the door after reversing the locks, without saying a word.

He didn't try to stop her. He set the locks and pulled off his shirt. What he needed was a shower and the same night's sleep he hoped she'd get.

The room was cold and empty.

But Kayla didn't take anything for granted. She put her stuff down, turned on all the lights, searched the bathroom, looked under the bed. Nobody waited for her.

She yawned and a wave of fatigue washed over her. She stripped and left her clothes and underwear in a pile and turned off all the lights and climbed under the covers of the soft bed.

On her back, she stared at the ceiling. Visions of Lori getting shot in the head filled her mind's eye. She watched her friend die several times and cursed because she'd been unable to help.

The life she thought was secure and orderly was upside down. She didn't know what to think or whom to believe anymore.

Dresnik a traitor?

It made no sense.

But what if Raven was correct? Had Dresnik been able to hide his dirty dealings for so long she never tripped to his behavior?

And why now? What was so important to Dixon King he'd let the lions out?

She couldn't think anymore, and she couldn't cry. Instead, she rolled over and tried to go to sleep, but the nightmares waiting kept her awake for a long time.

Raven finished his shower, dried off, and left the bathroom naked.

He sat on the edge of the bed. His eyes landed on the locket, on the dresser now, beside his wallet, keys and phone. He was always asked about the locket. He never answered the questions. Doing so only opened ancient wounds that refused to heal.

He hurt for Kayla Blaine. He'd lost friends in battle, too, but for cops, the hurt ran deeper than if they'd been soldiers expecting to die in battle. He and his late companions at least knew they were running on borrowed time, but cops didn't think the same way. They did their job, went home to their families, and hoped to live long enough to collect a pension. Raven had no such security net.

There was only so much in his power to accomplish for her. What he hoped to accomplish was to clear her of the current problems and deliver the justice Dixon King and Abelard Joulbert had avoided for so long. They had a long list of crimes to answer for, a long list of victims requiring vengeance.

Emotional involvement was forbidden. Despite how vulnerable he felt sometimes. Despite how vulnerable he knew Kayla must have felt. He could not get too close to her. There were things he needed to avoid, like the pain associated with attachment. There had been enough pain in his life already.

He turned off the lights and climbed into bed.

He'd get Kayla out of danger, dispatch the bad guys to their eternal judgement, and fade away.

Like always.

There were rules to follow, and he meant to follow them. Rule number one: no gunfights in public. Rule two: no roots. Don't even think about stopping the crusade. Too many lives rested on the justice dispensed from the barrel of his gun. If he tried to give it up, he'd only hear them screaming in his dreams.

And the screams would never stop until he died. One way or another. He hoped to end his life with his boots off but entertained no thoughts of such a demise actually happening. When his time came, there'd be a smoking gun in his hand, and a whole lot of bodies surrounding him.

He lay awake staring into space.

Then he heard a door in the hallway open and close.

Sleep eluded her.

Kayla flung the covers away, turned on the nightstand lamp, and dressed in a hurry. She looked at the hotel phone. Instinct screamed for her to call Captain Dresnik. Maybe seeing the captain in person made more sense. She'd feel better seeing him in a comfortable environment like Southern Station headquarters. She needed control. Right now, she had none, and the anxiety of being out of control flooded her with tension.

Jamming the key cards in a pocket of her jeans, she left the room and moved at a near run for the elevator. She decided to skip the elevator after all and pushed through the stairwell door.

Moments later, stepping onto the street, Kayla looked left and right. No traffic, no pedestrians. Real people were tucked safely away in their homes until the sun rose the next morning.

Going left, she headed for the Embarcadero. She might be able to flag down a passing cab and get to the Southern Station headquarters.

Kayla walked briskly, watching for any potential threat. Raven was right about one thing. Maybe she shouldn't be exposed outside. The safest place for her was headquarters surrounded by armed cops.

An arm snaked around her neck and pulled her off balance. A big hand wrapping around her mouth and muffled a scream.

CHAPTER SIXTEEN

Her frightened eyes locked on the face of Sam Raven.

"I thought you were supposed to be in bed," he said.

"Weren't you?"

She shoved, moving her head to get her mouth away from his hand. She landed a punch in his gut, and his hot breath struck her in the face as he backed away.

"Are you done?"

She breathed heavily.

"At the rate you're going, Kayla, I won't be able to help you at all."

She stared at him without a reply.

He reached for her. "Come on. Let's go—"

"Don't touch me!" She pulled away from his grasp.

"I'll go first," he said. "We're going inside, and we can sort this some more in the morning."

He turned on a heel. His shoes tapped on the sidewalk.

She closed her eyes and sighed. Who was she kidding? Trying to fight the tide was pointless. Right now, the tide was against her.

Kayla followed him into the hotel.

"She's gone."

Dixon King, dressed only in a kimono and ready for bed, cursed. He rose from the balcony lounge chair and opened the sliding glass door to his bedroom. He'd been enjoying the winking lights on the Golden Gate Bridge and quietly celebrating a good meeting with Joulbert. But his happiness rested on the evening's nightcap, the death of Kayla Blaine, and she was still alive.

"What do you mean *gone?*" King paced in front of his bed.

"As soon as the hit went down, somebody else showed up. One of my guys who survived said he wore all black and took out the two gunners on the sidewalk with a forty-five pistol. Before he passed out, he saw Blaine and this man run off."

"You try calling her?"

"No."

"Is this guy another cop? Friend?" King said.

"No clue."

"Any unknowns like this are going to wreck our plans, Dresnik."

"The unknowns began showing up after Charlie Kline was bailed out by a lawyer who doesn't appear to exist."

"Sam Raven."

"You saw it too?" Dresnik said.

"One of my guys. Think he's our man with the forty-five?"

"Probably."

"You dig up anything about his background?"

"Military record. 82nd Airborne. Overseas postings. Not much after. What about you?"

"All I have is rumor," King said. "He's either a bad guy or a good guy, and nobody is a hundred percent sure which. Not many seem to live long enough to comment directly."

"Did you ask Joulbert?"

"I don't want to bring him into this."

"He might have information. Maybe more than rumor. It can't hurt."

King said, "If he thinks we're under attack, he's—"

"What?"

"Never mind," King said. "He can't afford to pull out. It might not be a bad idea after all. I will ask him."

"Good."

"If Raven has Blaine," King said, "he has Kline tucked away too. Has there been any sign of Kline?"

Dresnik said, "We have him at two separate ATMs withdrawing the maximum allowed a few hours after he was released. Nothing since."

"The election is one week away. It's the wrong time to lose control."

"Looks like it all rests on this Raven fellow."

"You do your thing, I'll do mine. One of us needs to find him."

"I'm doing all I can."

"You need to do more, Dresnik. If we blow this, we lose. I've worked too hard to get this far to lose it because of your tiptoeing around trying not to get caught."

"If I get caught, who're you going to call from now on?"

"You'd be surprised who else I'd call."

Dresnik grunted.

"Is Peter York going to be the fall guy?"

"Who cares? Blaine killed him. We can say whatever we want."

King sighed. "Other than this call, today has been pretty good."

"I'm glad one of us is having a good night, Dixon."

King ended the call, opened a window and turned out the lights. Surprisingly, the sound of the ocean helped lull him to sleep.

Stephen Kennedy stood in the arrivals area of San Fran-cisco International Airport with a bouquet of roses. He waited for his wife Brooke.

He had come from an evening campaign meeting, so he still wore a suit. None of the other people waiting seemed to notice him. Even with his appearances on television, it amused him none of it seemed to make an impression.

Of course, not all who lived in the Bay Area gave one lick about politics in San Francisco. Who sat in the district attorney's office didn't affect them—unless they committed a crime in SF. The rest of the nine-county bay region gave it no thought whatsoever.

The lack of recognition bruised the ego, if Kennedy was honest. One good, high-profile case might be enough to elevate him to national recognition. Until then, he remained anonymous enough to collect his wife from the airport.

A flood of arriving passengers started down the escalator to the baggage area. He didn't see Brooke among them.

He still had thoughts of Melissa Doyle on his mind from their last romp. Nothing slowed her down, so he didn't slow down, either. With Brooke, he slowed down. He loved her, but she was a lousy lay. Unenthusiastic. Wouldn't try anything. She either wanted to be on the bottom or on top, depending on her mood, and usually not on top because she thought it made her face sag. It didn't sag. What did sag were her droopy middle-aged tits. They fell away from her body to hang on for dear life. Her idea of riding him was bouncing on his groin which more often than not crushed his balls and hurt.

The crowd of people stepped off the escalator and into the baggage claim area, greeting relatives with hugs and exclamations of excitement. The next flood of arriving passengers contained Brooke Kennedy.

She looked tired, especially around the eyes. She was a nervous flyer, and more than likely hadn't dozed on the plane. She wore her hair tied back, a wrinkled red blouse and tan skirt. The slung backpack over one shoulder probably contained her work computer and two or three historical romance novels. She read one after another like an addict. They filled her head with fantasies Kennedy couldn't bring to life. Real life was boring. Fiction was always better. Any unacknowledged cracks in their union worsened because she wished for fantasy rather than reality. Kennedy scowled at the flowers he held. A bouquet of roses was nice, but not enough to measure up to protagonists in a book.

He was getting angry with her and they hadn't even said hello yet.

If they were adult enough to address their issues, their relationship would be different. Kennedy's problem was he didn't know where to start, and Brooke refused to talk.

Kennedy took a deep breath. Now wasn't the time to think of their problems.

She approached him with a weak smile. "Hi."

She leaned forward and he gave her a peck on the cheek.

"Thank you for the flowers, wow," she said, taking the bouquet in her free left hand. "They smell wonderful!"

"How many bags do you have?"

"Only the one."

They moved to the appropriate carousel and watched the bags come up the chute and onto the conveyer.

"Green one?" he said.

"No, the new purple one. I think the side got torn on the way."

Finally, the new purple suitcase with a small rip on the side rounded the carousel. Kennedy grabbed the handle, extended it to let it roll across the floor, and pulled the suitcase behind him. The small wheels on the bottom moved smoothly on the bright tiled floor.

"How was the conference?"

"Boring. Mostly doctors goofing off and drinking."

She sold equipment for a medical device company. The conference had been a trade show to display new gear for doctors and hospital officials.

"Nice hotel?" he asked.

"Bed was lumpy."

"Sorry to hear that."

They reached the parking structure and took an elevator to an upper level. He'd parked the white Lexus coupe under some lights. As they approached, he once again marveled at the sleek design. It was one heck of a car. He might have to sell it when he became DA. It might not be proper for a representative of the people to have a flashy ride. Plus, he could use city vehicles to get around; with drivers, a better option.

He accelerated onto the freeway heading for their home in Daly City. She knew about the condo in San Francisco. Supposedly, it was for out-of-town partners of his firm to stay when they visited. She had no idea he actually used it as his love nest.

Once inside the house, Brooke set her backpack on the kitchen table. She trimmed the stems of the roses over the sink and put them in a vase with water.

Kennedy set the suitcase in the bedroom for her to attend to later.

They talked briefly about the state of the campaign as she brushed her teeth and removed her makeup. Kennedy leaned in the doorway of the bathroom, watching his wife, and talking too fast. The latest *Chronicle* poll showing him three points ahead of Brandt pleased her. She supported his campaign but didn't seem excited about it. Kennedy wondered if she feared he might try and run for higher office later on. It was another thing they didn't talk about, creating yet another crack in their bond.

After a while they climbed into bed and she rolled onto her side. He moved closer, rubbed her back, and suggested they fool around a bit.

"Not tonight," she said.

He rolled over. He had a question-and-answer fundraiser early the next afternoon, lunch provided by the sponsor, and a full night's sleep was a good idea.

CHAPTER SEVENTEEN

Danielle Rawlings rinsed the soap from her body, her hands moving along the curves of her hips and flat of her stomach as the suds ran down the shower drain.

She couldn't help but admire her body, nice and tight and round where it should be. She'd taken the summer off and put on a few pounds and it had been a hard couple of months taking them off again. It wasn't as easy post-30 to shrink.

Today was the beginning of the biggest payday she'd seen in the last ten years. Normally she demanded such a high price—two-thousand bucks for a one-hour minimum—she only needed to see a few clients a week to maintain her lifestyle. She added an extra client or two a week when she wanted new shoes.

Her latest client was a woman.

Chelsea Brandt.

Danielle wasn't sure how Chelsea had found her. She mentioned in the phone call a "mutual friend" who knew of her work, and their conversation after didn't last long. "Mutual friend" might mean a lot of things, but to Danielle, it meant a shadow client. Somebody who wanted to remain hidden. It was probably the same shadow client who had hired her for jobs before through various cutouts, always in San Francisco. Honey trap jobs. She didn't question anything. If she tried, it was a sure-fire way to get hurt.

Chelsea needed to set a honey trap for a target susceptible to such things.

Target: Stephen Kennedy, Brandt's opponent in the DA race.

The thrill of getting involved in the shady side of politics made her accept the job. She'd studied political science in college, knew the history of various scandals; not only contributing, but keeping it quiet without making the mistakes of others, was a challenge she couldn't resist.

Danielle could have chosen a normal career, but one night back in college, at a frat party, a guy kept making moves on her. He wouldn't stop despite her protests, and she finally told him if he wanted to spend time with her it would cost $200. To her surprise, the dude agreed. And he wasn't bad in bed. Over and done and he never bothered her again. Then she started getting ideas on how to make more money than any normal job would pay her. She only had to use what she'd been born with to make it happen.

Future transactions had been simple too. She still finished her degree, though. Maybe someday she'd want to quit escorting. The nest egg in her bank account wasn't large enough yet. A little more, and she'd consider other options.

She stepped out of the shower onto the bathmat, toweling off and blow drying her hair. She waved the hot air over the rest of her body. The heat felt good. When she could run fingers through her dry black hair, she turned off the device and set it on the cluttered counter. A girl needed product, and lots of it, and while the mess might be an eyesore, she knew where each item resided.

Her outfit waited on the bed. She wasn't a resident of San

Francisco, and Brandt had put her up in a fancy hotel. She actually lived in Nevada where one could be an escort without fear of the cops. She managed to avoid dangerous clients by making sure only the wealthy could afford her time.

The hotel suite was a large one, bedroom separate from a sunken living room. Wide balcony and a 60-inch flat screen and soft leather furnishings. Who wanted to work when one could lounge in such a nice place? With room service, she'd never have to leave, and could sit around in her pajamas all day. But she wasn't getting paid to binge watch *90 Day Fiancé*.

Perfect place for an off-the-books tryst, too, but that wouldn't be appropriate. She had a client, and the client's needs always came first. This wasn't her first job outside Nevada. She'd often thought about taking her act on the road, advertising through the various escort websites, but doing so invited too much trouble. Travel expenses would eat into her profit margin, too. Better to stay in Nevada where the law wouldn't bother her, and she could have better control over the clientele. But for Chelsea Brandt's "friend" and the paycheck associated with the effort, she was willing to make an exception.

Her outfit was conservative, simple white blouse and black skirt, stockings, black heels. In keeping with her naughty side, she had black leather underwear to finish the ensemble. She'd apply light makeup and tie back her black hair in a ponytail. Kennedy struck her as somebody who might like the proverbial girl next door, so she wanted to dress for the part.

She tossed her hair some more before tying it and applied her makeup in light strokes. Nothing heavy. She didn't need it. Danielle only splurged on the lipstick. The bright red contrasted with her creamy white skin.

She didn't like her nose. It was too narrow and ended in a point, a rounded point, but it looked hideous, nonetheless. She also didn't want to alter it. She didn't like doctors' offices or needles. She only visited medical professionals when she needed to, and she didn't think a nose job fit the requirement. None of her clients seemed to mind. They were more interested in the rest of her.

She slipped her feet into black six-inch stilettos and then the crowning piece of her wardrobe. Black spike earrings. They sparkled for a little bling, suggested a dark side, and matched her shoes. They also matched her underwear. Stephen Kennedy wouldn't discover that secret right away.

And there was a dark side to the whole thing. Instead of getting off, she might get killed. Because, yeah, she knew the history of certain political shenanigans, suspected the identity of Chelsea Brandt's "friend" and such friends made people disappear without a trace if the participants messed up.

CHAPTER EIGHTEEN

Melissa Doyle said, "Don't be nervous."

Stephen Kennedy adjusted his tie for the umpteenth time. "My wife is home."

"Is that it? I thought it was the sharks waiting in the audience."

"Those people I can handle."

They stood in the office of the restaurant manager who had opened his banquet room for the Q&A event. Stephen Kennedy was about to address a bunch of rich people, tech CEOs with their own celebrity following. He had to convince them to not only give him money but provide an endorsement.

Kennedy dropped his hands and looked Melissa Doyle up and down. Her pantsuit fit her curves and left no doubt she knew she looked good.

He thought about locking the door for a quickie, but business first.

The morning edition of the *Chronicle* still showed him a couple of points ahead, but Brandt was closing in. Too close for comfort with less than a week out. A few key endorsements from the tech sector might help widen the gap in his favor.

"Do I look okay?" he said.

She smoothed the front of his suit coat. "You look fine."

Melissa Doyle leaned in for a kiss and he took the opportunity. It was long and wet and held the promise of something more, but much later. He pinched her rear and she squealed, pulling away, laughing. She wagged a finger at him.

"No more, we're working."

He smiled. "Let's go raise some money."

Stephen Kennedy wasn't nervous anymore.

The restaurant served chicken in a delicious cream sauce, Caesar salad on the side, with steamed vegetables. At least it wasn't typical catered "rubber chicken", which may have robbed Kennedy of a joke. The audience wouldn't have attended if they knew the meal would be sub-par.

After the meal, Kennedy stood up at the head table and addressed the audience. He recognized many faces from local and national news. They were all billionaires. He'd never spoken to so much money in his life.

His opening speech was short, and Melissa Doyle, with a microphone, fielded random questions. Kennedy seemed to answer satisfactorily based on the happy reactions he received. This crowd wanted a safe San Francisco. Kennedy stressed it was his primary goal to create as safe a city as possible. They wanted to hold conferences in the city, attract business from around the country. They didn't need their visitors afraid to go out at night, or watch homeless people crap on the sidewalk. The city had recently lost several out-of-town conventions because of the filth.

The pitch didn't work on everybody, but enough lined up after the Q&A to write checks. Kennedy thanked each one as they passed their checks to members of his staff at a side table. Melissa Doyle stood nearby, beaming at him.

One CEO, a roly-poly dude who insisted on wearing un-flattering tight clothes, held up the line, but at the end of the conversation, wrote the biggest check. He departed with a much younger and thinner woman, and Kennedy shook his head. Money made up for any feature an individual lacked.

One woman in particular caught Kennedy's attention. White blouse, black skirt, hair in a ponytail. Her black earrings jumped out at him. He had to keep his eyes on hers, but had he been allowed to roam a little, he knew he would not have been disappointed in the view on display.

"I'm happy to contribute," she said, shaking Kennedy's hand.

"I didn't get your name."

"It's Danielle. I run a small software company you've never heard of. We make apps."

"Uh-huh."

"Anyway, my office is on Townsend, and it gets a little dicey there sometimes. I like knowing we'll get more police presence."

Patrol coverage in questionable areas, where some of the tech companies had offices because of cheaper rent, had been a recurring question.

"I will do all I can to make sure your employees are protected, Danielle."

She smiled. People liked the sound of their own name.

"Maybe we can discuss it further. You know, in private." She pulled a business card from a small purse. "We can sched-ule later." She flicked the tip of her tongue under her upper lip.

He glanced around, took the card.

"Of course."

He smiled. Melissa Doyle didn't see the exchange. Her back was to him as she gave instructions to one of the other staffers.

"Well," she said, "until then." She flashed him a bright smile and pivoted and melted into the crowd. Kennedy's attention turned to the next donor, so he didn't get to watch her leave. He figured the view would have been as nice as the front.

Nobody could drive in San Francisco holding a cell phone. Danielle Rawlings made sure her hands-free earpiece was plugged into the phone when she called Chelsea Brandt's private line. Stuck at a light, she watched a MUNI bus negotiate a tight corner while avoiding a skinny teenager on a skateboard who cut in front of the bus.

"Yes?"

"It's me," Danielle said. "Lunch was wonderful."

"Contact made?"

"Contact hooked. Big time. Only a matter of setting up the rest."

"He'll want to take you to his condo, but we need you to steer him to another place."

"No problem."

"We'll have it set up by the end of the day."

"Let me know when and I'll make the kill."

Chelsea Brandt ended the call and Danielle plucked the Bluetooth from her ear and set it in a cup holder. It wasn't even two o'clock yet, and she had nothing to do until Chelsea Brandt called. Plenty of time to put her pajamas on, park on the couch, and do some binge watching on the big television.

Maybe room service could bring up some wine.

She hoped her little tongue trick drew Kennedy into her web. He was good looking. She might have done the honey trap free if she knew he was such a hunk.

It amused her he had worked so hard not to drop his eyes, but a chill ran through her. She hoped, hoped, *hoped* he hadn't been staring at her nose.

CHAPTER NINETEEN

The calm wind was a huge plus.

Dixon King watched two of his people set out trays of cold cuts, condiments, and sourdough bread. He'd invited Abelard Joulbert over for lunch. He needed to admit some of the issues they faced and get the Frenchman's input.

The chief of the house guard, Wayne, stood at the other end of the balcony. The rising towers of the Golden Gate Bridge touched the sky in the distance. Boats in the bay added more attraction. Two sailboats seemed to be racing, currently neck and neck, the churning wake behind them testifying to the speed at which they traveled.

Now and then, cruise ships from other piers traveled to the ocean via the Golden Gate, but King didn't know of any scheduled to do so today. It might have been a nice bonus if one had. The big ships were always fun to watch.

The shimmering water looked like glass despite the ripples of the waves. The afternoon temperature was perfect; not too hot, not too cold, no jacket required.

Alcatraz in the distance. Maybe they could make jokes about ending up there. King laughed to himself.

Leonard Wexler, wearing black as usual, escorted Abelard

Joulbert onto the balcony. He excused himself with Wayne in tow. The rest of the guards around the house, the ones with the artillery, were out of sight.

He'd set aside some food for Wexler in the kitchen. King waved a hand over the spread, and Joulbert dug in, building a tall sandwich slathered with mayo and mustard. King offered either beer or sparkling water, and Joulbert selected a bottle of beer.

"This is a lovely view," Joulbert said. His sandwich was a mix of each meat offered on the plate, and he must have detected King liked the pastrami, because he'd only used two slices.

"It cost me a lot," King said. "And it costs a lot to keep running."

"We don't have views like this where I come from."

"When our deal is finalized, you're welcome to spend as much time here as you think you require."

Joulbert grinned. "Maybe I'll make up excuses."

"There are plenty of spare bedrooms for any guests, too."

"That's kind of you."

They ate quietly. King hadn't gone cheap on the cold cuts. The cuts of roast beef were thick and lean; the turkey also; and of course, extra pastrami.

The hot peppers were also his idea. Fresh potato salad complemented the sandwiches. Plastic covering shielded the food from any flies who might come along since the wind was calm. Usually, the high winds kept them away. It also kept King from using the balcony for meals. It was no fun watching your food fly away. He wasn't worried about seagulls, who mostly kept to the coastal edge and especially Fort Point near the SF side of the bridge.

The two men chatted about small things, nothing related to business, and King brought up *The Problems*. Joulbert listened quietly, continued eating, and waited for King to finish.

When he did, Joulbert only shrugged.

"As I said the other night, we all have our concerns and worries. Setting up our arrangement could never have gone off without a hitch. I admire what you've done so far, and if we work together, we can iron out the wrinkles."

"I appreciate your response."

"This Inspector Blaine is the last one to be an issue?"

"Her and the reporter, but we have his stuff. In fact, my man Wexler is working on tying up a loose end mentioned in one of the reporter's notes."

"And this Sam Raven?"

"Your guess is as good as mine. My police contact turned up a military record, and my inquiries only gave me a bunch of rumors. I need facts. Does he mean anything to you?"

"I know the name."

"You know the *name*, do you know the man?"

"Nobody knows the man. You're right, some don't know if he's with us or with the law. Personally, I think he's only out for himself."

"What do you mean?"

"He's a man with a vendetta. An unknown vendetta. Nobody understands why he's going around playing avenger. But he searches out victims of crime or sticks his nose in things when he finds them."

"How would he have learned about our business?"

Joulbert shrugged. "My organization has been taking a lot of hits, as you're aware. It's possible one of my people told him. We had one, a man named Dimitri, vanish on us. I'd had a tail on him, on several people actually, to see who was telling the cops about our business. Dimitri did meet somebody who could have been Raven, but my surveillance people didn't know for sure."

"Nobody knows what he looks like?"

"Nobody who does see his face usually lives long enough to draw a picture."

"I'm getting a picture myself," King said. He looked out at the water. Such a peaceful sight did not bring any peace to the thunder rising in his spirit at the moment.

They had a man in the mix who answered to nobody, worked for himself, and nobody knew what he looked like. Rumors again. No facts. How could somebody like Wexler be expected to find Sam Raven if they didn't know where to start?

"The woman remains the key," King decided.

Joulbert swallowed a mouthful of beer. "I agree."

"We know what she looks like, she'll have to come up for air at some point, and when we find her, we'll find *him*."

"There's still something we lack," Joulbert said.

"What?"

"A place to start. Where has he hidden this woman Blaine?"

"I think she'll stay with him. He needs a guide around the city. She'll know things."

"You mentioned a loose end a second ago."

"The one Wexler is looking for, yeah. A transient mentioned in Kline's notes. He apparently talked to the hooker we used to give Whitlow his overdose. He might get ideas."

"Transients don't often—"

King held up a hand to cut Joulbert off. "I'm not taking any chances."

"What if Blaine and Raven are looking for this man too?"

King snapped his fingers. "I'm glad you came over today, Abelard. *That* is exactly the kind of thinking we need."

CHAPTER TWENTY

"This isn't the kind of car for this neighborhood," Kayla said.

"I don't disagree," said Raven.

"Those guys over there? They're waiting for you to park so they can try and boost this thing."

"You sure they aren't thinking of carjacking?"

She laughed. "Both of us armed?"

"It would be the last mistake they ever made."

"You and I might get along yet," she said.

"A while ago you called me a murderer."

"There's a difference when somebody's trying to kill you first."

"How do you know the story of my life doesn't include plenty of self-defense?"

"You've made it clear you're not ever telling me the story of your life."

"It's boring anyway," he said.

"Try me."

"Here's a parking spot."

"I'm telling you we shouldn't be doing this."

"It's a rental. I signed for extra insurance."

The Tenderloin sat in the ritzy area of the southern side of Nob Hill. It lay smack between the shopping mecca at Union Square and the Civic Center to the southwest. Fifty square blocks. More crime per square mile than the rest of the city combined, almost all of it drug related. Predators roamed; homeless squatted; social services struggled to cope. The boundary between rich and poor was nothing more than a few steps. Cross a street and go from squalor to prosperity. It was in this mess Raven had failed to find the man named Hank a few nights ago. With Kayla's help, he hoped for a better result tonight.

Raven locked the BMW at the curb. An empty lot sat behind them. Whatever building had sat there before was long gone, replaced by charred debris. A fire had burned down the building. The structures on either side had wooden boards for windows; gang graffiti covered the walls.

They started walking.

"This is a needle in a haystack," Kayla said. She walked fast to keep up with Raven's long strides.

"We have to find him. He witnessed enough to tell Charlie Kline, and that convinced Kline to contact you. The entire case may hinge on what this man Hank saw."

"I thought you only shot people."

He stopped, blocking her path with an arm, locking her eyes with his. "You continue to misunderstand me, *Kayla*, and I'm getting tired of it."

She backed up a step. "All right. I'm sorry."

He pivoted and started walking again. Her shoes scraped on the sidewalk as she hurried to keep up.

The bright streetlamps brought the section of the neighborhood to life in long shadows. Lines of cars parked curbside; homeless lying flat against buildings, sometimes one on either side of the sidewalk, making navigation tight. They ignored pleas for money. The open dice games in alleys or people jamming needles into their arms in doorways and alcoves also faded behind them. They watched for broken and stray needles on the ground.

Raven noted the old buildings, some with the ancient fire escapes outside the windows. Lots of brick and faded paint.

"He's not going to be in any of the fancier bars," Kayla said.

"I can't believe anybody comes here for fun."

"You'd be surprised. Arts, theater, it's all here. Some of it of the seedier variety, like the Mitchell Brothers' over there. Still the gold standard in adult entertainment in this area."

"Didn't one brother shoot the other over money?"

"Something like that. I was working vice at the time but didn't get the case."

"We need to hit the dive bars," Raven said.

"Or start looking under these blankets and asking if anybody knows him."

Raven didn't like those odds. He'd meant what he said. A lot rested on Hank's information. They didn't have Kline's material, so they needed the original source. It would have been easy for Raven to go scorched earth and wipe out King and Joulbert. But with good cops dead and innocents in the crossfire, he needed evidence to explain all the dead bodies. There *would* be dead bodies in the end. He also wanted Kayla Blaine and Charlie Kline free and clear, the traitor in the SFPD's Southern Station dealt with, and as much of the corruption cleared out of the city as possible.

Always the impossible dream, but if he dreamed big, he might get a slice of the pie.

Kayla led Raven to three dive bars, where nobody seemed to know who Hank was. They asked people on the street. Raven regretted not having a description, but it might not have helped. The homeless men they found had the same general appearance. Dirty clothes, long hair, and beards.

After the fourth bar, Raven noticed they'd picked up a tail.

"Three guys are following us."

Kayla didn't look back. "I'm sure you can handle it, cowboy."

Raven bit off his reply. They shook the tail by extending their walk and extra block, cutting between buildings. After a while, they backtracked to their destination.

The fifth bar sat below street level in the basement of an abandoned tenement.

The bartender knew somebody named Hank. He pointed to a man slouched in a corner with a beer and two shots of home brew whiskey the bar sold cheap. Raven identified himself, mentioned Charlie Kline. The man acknowledged he knew Charlie. Raven asked if they could talk outside. Hank said okay, downed both shots, and attacked the mug of beer. He drained the glass in a series of swallows and when he set the mug down, didn't belch.

Kayla took the lead as they returned to the sidewalk, gesturing to the alley next door where Raven led Hank.

"What happened to Charlie?" Hank said.

He was shorter than Raven, but almost as tall as Kayla. His long hair, spotted with dirt, looked gray in the glare of a nearby streetlamp.

"He's out of the city," Raven said.

"I saw the police got him."

Kayla said, "We got him out."

He looked at her. "Who are you?"

She showed him her police badge. "I'm the inspector Charlie called after he talked to you."

"Where's Margot?"

"Margot is dead, Hank," Kayla said. "That's why we need to talk to you. We need to know what you told Charlie."

"Margot worked my corner," Hank said.

"What do you mean?" Raven said.

"I'm there begging, she's there hooking."

"Simple enough," Raven said. "Who talked to her?"

"Somebody picked her up in a big fancy car," Hank said. "She was gone about ten minutes. When the car brought her back, she told me somebody wanted her to give Whitlow cocaine. She was supposed to be somewhere the next night so he could pick her up. Her job was to make sure he picked her up."

"Did you see anybody in the car?" Kayla said.

"No. It was a Lincoln like my daddy used to have, but newer."

"Why would she tell you all this, Hank?" Raven said.

"They gave her a thousand-dollar bill," Hank said. "She quit for the night. Who isn't going to talk about a thousand-dollar bill?"

"In this neighborhood?" Raven said.

"We take care of each other," Hank said. "Some of us, anyway. Nobody else gives a damn."

Kayla looked up and down the street while Raven talked.

"Did they give her the cocaine?" Raven said.

"She was supposed to get it from somebody named Billy."

"Where do I find this Billy?"

"Morgue, probably."

"He's dead?"

"Somebody shot him the other night. Took half his face clean off."

Raven bit his tongue. His handiwork. He'd blasted a lead he hadn't known was a lead.

Nice going, cowboy.

Kayla said, "Raven—"

He turned his head in the direction she indicated.

"Raven, get down!"

Raven grabbed the front of Hank's coat, pulling the man with him toward the ground as two shots split the air. Kayla, running to a parked car, braced her gun on the trunk as she returned fire.

Two men converged on the alley from across the street. Kayla fired twice and stopped one of the thugs in his tracks. The man toppled onto the street. The second continued, leaping over the trunk of the car as Kayla shifted her aim. Before she could fire, the big man collided with her, falling hard on top of her as they hit the sidewalk.

Raven jumped up and the movement on his left caught his attention first. He pivoted as a third shooter, squatting low between two parked cars, aimed a pistol. He didn't want a gunfight in public. He took out his leather sap and charged at the shooter.

He was a big man, broad in the shoulders, and dressed in black. The man's aim did not waver, but Raven did not hesitate in spite of the muzzle pointed in his direction. He raised the sap and prepared to launch himself at the shooter's neck.

The man in black fired twice, the rounds missing Raven, and Raven leaped. The man in black rose to run. Raven collided with him and they tumbled into the street as a car rushed by, missing them. The road blacktop felt dry and rough, Raven trying to roll the man beneath him. His opponent struggled to get his handgun between them.

Raven struck with the sap. He hit the man's gun arm, the man screamed, the gun falling from his grasp. He punched Raven in the face. Stunned, Raven's reaction slowed as the big man threw him off. Raven slammed slamming against the fender of the car behind him.

The man in black sprang to his feet and took off across the intersection. Cars screeched, one almost smacking him in the legs. For a big fellow, he moved fast, skirting the vehicle to reach the other side of the street.

Kayla screamed again.

Raven, despite pain racing through his body, scrambled to his feet. He grabbed the fallen sap and ran to Kayla.

The second shooter had Kayla pinned under his bulk. The fist at the end of his thick arm slammed into her face, once, twice. Raven grabbed the man by the cuff of his shirt, pulling him off Kayla to bash him on the side of the head. The sap landed with a loud *thwack*.

Kayla rolled out from under the goon, who didn't fall unconscious from the blow. Raven raised the sap again, but the goon slammed his left fist into Raven's gut instead. Breath left Raven as he doubled over, turning away.

As Raven hit the ground, Kayla turned her SIG Sauer P229 loose. One shot, another, as the goon shuffled away along the sidewalk. He cut across the street.

Raven groaned. "My goodness," he said, spitting. "Do they build them out of steel here?"

Kayla helped him to his feet. She had a cut under her left eye already leaking a teardrop of blood. "Are you okay?"

"He didn't hit too hard," she said.

"Made of steel indeed." Raven stowed the sap and looked at Hank on the ground.

He was beyond help. The two shots Raven believed the big man fired at him had actually struck Hank. The homeless man remained on the ground. He wouldn't be rising again. A pool of blood spread below him.

Kayla cursed. Raven pushed her forward. "Come on, there's nothing we can do."

Witnesses rose from hiding and yelled for others to come and see what happened. None seemed too interested in Raven and Kayla as they made their escape and cut down another alley. Hank had said the neighborhood watched out for each other. Perhaps Hank would get the sendoff he deserved.

They reached the BMW 530i. The car had remained unmolested during their trek. Raven started the motor and executed a U-turn.

Kayla examined her face in the mirror of the passenger visor. With tissues from her purse, she put pressure on the cut.

"You sure you're okay?"

"I have bony cheeks," she said. "Dude's hand is going to be killing him tomorrow."

"If the headache doesn't do him in first."

"True," she agreed.

"Nice bit of shooting with the first goon."

"I wish I'd seen the third. Those first two were a distraction."

"Yes, poor Hank."

"Did you get a look at the killer?"

"Dressed in black. Crew cut. Looked like—"

"A brick wall?"

"Yeah."

"Leonard Wexler. Dixon King's number two."

"Those two are officially on the playing field."

"Was there a doubt?"

"Not for me," Raven said. "What about you?"

"I'm convinced."

"Afraid it does nothing for evidence purposes, though."

"I'm more worried about Charlie."

"If he left the city like I told him, he's fine. If not, he's in danger too."

"I didn't see your big bad forty-five."

"Rule number one. No gunfights in public."

"Are you kidding me?"

"Too many people could get hurt."

"Somebody *did* get hurt, Raven. Somebody else got killed."

Raven gripped the steering wheel until his hands hurt. Maybe she had a point. Could he have prevented Hank's murder with a blast from the Nighthawk? He'd thought the gun had been turned on him. Usually rushing somebody pointing a gun at you surprised the daylights out of the person holding the gun. It hadn't worked this time. Either Raven had miscalculated and cost Hank his life, or Leonard Wexler wasn't like anybody he'd faced before.

He wasn't sure what to think. Maybe he could have prevented Hank's death. Maybe not. Maybe he'd have missed and hit a bystander.

He didn't know the answer. His rules had never failed him before. He decided the answer was to stick with the rules and put the shooting in the category of *shit happens*.

Kayla flipped up the visor. "What a mess."

"We'll get it cleaned up, Kayla."

"You promise...Sam?"

"It's what I'm good at." He smiled. "What happens after? That's a different story. Between the two of us we'll figure this out."

"We will," she said.

Raven drove. He smiled in spite of Hank's loss. Kayla seemed to be thawing. A little action together might have done the trick.

He'd made a big promise, he had to admit. Raven hoped he didn't fail Kayla Blaine like he had failed so many others.

Like he had failed Hank.

Neither spoke for the rest of the ride to the hotel.

CHAPTER TWENTY-ONE

It was about to be a twofer night for Leonard Wexler.

Still catching his breath from his run from the alley where he'd nailed the snitch named Hank, he drove his burbling black Challenger out of the Tenderloin toward Geary Street. He was a little pissed he'd have to report to King they'd lost a man in the process, but at least achieved the main goal.

Then his phone chirped.

Wexler, who didn't need a traffic ticket, grabbed a wireless earbud from a cup holder. He pushed it into his ear and answered.

"What is it?"

"Hey," one of his guys said, "we found the reporter. Got eyes on him as we speak."

"Where?"

"Little rat trap motel near Beale Street."

"Stay on him," Wexler said. "I'll be there as soon as I can." Wexler hung up and calculated the distance. Close to two miles, maybe forty-five minutes with traffic.

He called King as he made a left on Post heading for Mission Street. The boss would want to know about the man he saw Kayla Blaine with who was the mysterious

Sam Raven.

He ignored the pain in his right arm where Raven had struck with the sap. He had to give the man credit. He had no fear running toward the barrel of a gun. A man like that wasn't normal.

He was dangerous.

Very very dangerous.

Wexler knew when they faced each other again, he'd have to be the one to shoot first.

Room service knocked at 7:45 a.m. the next morning as requested. Raven, dressed for the day, answered the door and the waiter wheeled in a cart with breakfast for two. Raven made no excuse why he was alone in the room, and the waiter didn't ask. Raven gave him a $5 and the waiter departed.

Raven shut the door and pushed the cart to the table. He called Kayla to tell her breakfast had arrived.

He lifted the lids from the plates and set the food out on the table, with napkins and cutlery, adding the sealed plastic cups of orange juice and the decanter of hot coffee. He'd requested tea for himself, the hot water contained in a metal pot. He poured a cup and dropped a bag of Earl Grey English Breakfast into the water.

He added the selection of creamer packs to the table, checked the cart for more, and pushed it aside.

Even on the road, Raven insisted on a proper table setting. It made him feel normal.

The punch in the face from the night before still smarted a little and banging against a car hadn't done his left shoulder any good. He had a nice bruise there. But all in all, he'd made out okay. Still ticking.

But the results still haunted him. For now, he had to push on and deal with the consequences later. There would be plenty of consequences to sort out in the end. If they survived.

By the time she knocked five minutes later, he presented the nice table, and she smiled.

"Smells great," she said. "Sorry I haven't showered yet."

She'd tied up her hair and, without makeup, the growing bruise on her left cheek was obvious. She didn't dwell on it. She dug into her scrambled eggs and bacon while Raven finally savored the all-meat omelet. The buttered wheat toast and hash browns made the meal perfect.

Raven turned on the morning news despite Kayla's protests.

"Let's have a quiet morning," she said.

"I need to know what's going on."

"It's the same mess as always."

Raven smiled and lowered the sound. She turned her chair so her back was to the television and bent over her plate some more.

Presently Raven stopped eating and stared at the television.

"What?"

"They found Charlie Kline."

She turned her chair.

Footage of the police pulling a body from one of the piers ran while the anchor talked about cops finding the reporter's body. The camera couldn't get close enough to the crowd of cops to get a clear shot of the body, but Raven had no reason to doubt the story.

She turned to him. "You said—"

"He must not have listened to me."

Raven looked down at his partially eaten omelet, pieces of sausage, bacon, and ham spilling out of the cut in the egg. Refusing to eat wouldn't resurrect Kline, and he needed his strength. He resumed eating, but slower, and didn't enjoy the food as much.

The cost was increasing each day. The situation was going to boil over, out of control. Raven needed a way to take control and fast.

"They're tying off loose ends," she said.

"They haven't killed you yet."

Her sharp look froze him. "You expect them to succeed?"

"Not as long as I'm here."

"I feel safer already."

Raven wasn't sure if she was being sarcastic or telling the truth. He turned off the television.

"You should never have turned it on," she said.

He ate some more, took a bite of toast, and sipped his black tea.

"Who could King's DA candidate be?" Raven said.

"It's one or the other."

"But which?" he said.

"My money's on Brandt."

"Why?"

"She's been in the city government longer," Kayla said. "She already knows about the graft. She knows who the players are. It would be easier to recruit her than try for a green pea like Kennedy."

"We need a way to find out which one is dirty." He ate some more. "What about Wexler?"

"What about him?"

"King needs to communicate with his candidate. Maybe he uses Wexler as a runner."

"Good idea."

Raven smiled, but there was no light behind his eyes. Kline's death, and Hank's death, weighed on him. He was losing people fast. If he lost Kayla too, it was game over.

Kayla watched Raven eat. He seemed distracted, pre-occupied, almost afraid. His attitude had changed after the news of Kline's death. She didn't blame him. The events of the previous night put him in a dark place. Kline's death pushed him further into his dark place.

She had no idea how he'd recover, but suspected he'd plow through like a professional. She hoped.

Kayla chewed a piece of bacon. She was growing to trust him after last night's adventure in the Tenderloin, despite the tragedy. She swallowed some coffee.

She hadn't gone straight to sleep the previous night, or morning, whatever it was, and felt embarrassed about lying awake fantasizing about the man who'd pulled a thug off of her and bashed him over the head. What might he be like as a lover? What would it feel like to have that toned body on top of hers? They were crazy thoughts. She was going through a challenging period, her emotions a roller coaster, and she knew deep down she was only objectifying Raven because he seemed like something stable in a world gone mad. It was hero worship and nothing more.

She had to stay focused and think of the case. Solving the case was the most important thing.

Once she solved the mystery behind District Attorney Whitlow's death and prevented Dixon King from accomplishing whatever goals he had in mind with the French, life could return to a pattern resembling normality. Well, after she saluted her dead friends.

She noted she hadn't thought of the traitor in the department in her rundown.

It was still too much to consider. Somebody close to her, somebody she'd served with, didn't care if she lived or died as long as he or she received King's dirty money in exchange.

She didn't think Raven was a bad guy, but wasn't entirely certain he was a good guy, either. She was comfortable enough with gray areas to give him a pass, but cautiously so.

It all depended on how he recovered himself.

Her skin still felt sweaty under the clothes she'd thrown on after the breakfast call. What she needed was a shower, some makeup over the bruise, and more coffee. She had easy access to coffee, so one problem solved. She downed what was in her mug and reached for the decanter for a refill.

CHAPTER TWENTY-TWO

After breakfast, Kayla returned to her room to shower. Before she left, Raven told her he'd be taking a walk around the hotel.

He had some thinking to do.

Looking for Leonard Wexler, as he and his crew searched for them, was a good idea. If Raven knew King, and he knew many like him, he'd be protected behind walls, with more men and guns within those walls, but Wexler could lead Raven straight through the labyrinth if he had the proper leverage. Or Raven could leave him on the street and send the kind of message the mafia chief would understand without fail.

He had another idea, the germ of which stretched back to his conversation with Charlie Kline. Oscar Morey still hadn't come through with information on Tyrone Biggins, whom Kline revealed as his source. He was still worth going after and exploiting. If Raven could get him to turn state's evidence, they could take him to the FBI to explain all the bodies. The SFPD was a losing proposition. Federal involvement was the only solution.

Raven added the idea to his list.

He wandered through the second-floor lounge with its

high ceiling, one side with floors lined with rooms, the other nothing but steel frame and tinted glass, offering a view of the busy Embarcadero and bay beyond. There was a bar at the far end, along with a glass elevator overlooking the floor. Raven imagined watching the carpet drop away as the elevator car ascended.

Raven ignored the bar and stopped in front of the tinted glass to watch the road. Traffic flowed on green lights and stacked up on reds. Rail cars traveled along tracks down the center of the roadway. The bay offered the usual water view, but Raven didn't examine it. He preferred to keep his eyes on the traffic.

He wondered what Kayla must be feeling. Alone probably. Most likely tired, and maybe in a little bit of pain from the blows of the previous night. He knew all too well what that felt like. He admired her toughness. It was an attribute he noticed most people possessed without realizing they had such power; unfortunately, it only manifested under extreme stress.

Like somebody trying to kill you.

As often as he thought it would be nice to have somebody like Kayla by his side while on his crusade, he knew it wasn't possible. He didn't want somebody taken from him again. His goal was to make sure she could return to her normal life, despite the incidents making such a return far from normal— she'd be without dear friends who had fallen on the front line. There might forever after be a hint of trauma behind her eyes, but she'd adjust, somehow.

He watched the traffic some more. A bus rumbled through the flow.

Charlie Kline. *Poor chap.* Raven knew why he had stayed. Kline was made of tough stuff, too, otherwise he wouldn't have taken the risks he took to try and get his story to the public. Running away meant he was a coward, and he wasn't the kind of person who could look himself in the mirror if he ran away, no matter the circumstances.

He'd stayed to try and find a way to help on his own. Raven had no idea if he had planned to make contact a second time.

Killing Kline had been a calculated move on King's part. He'd spared the man's life early on because of the attention such a murder would draw. Now that his plans were in full motion, he had another problem: Raven and Kayla. Exit Kline to push Raven and Kayla into isolation, where they had nowhere to run. They knew the police would be no help because not only was Kayla's Southern Station leadership compromised, but the leadership of the *entire* SFPD was compromised. They'd be forced to give up or hide and be easy pickings for an assassin like Wexler.

It was a lousy spot to be in, but Raven had been in tighter corners before.

He'd usually blasted his way out of them.

And there might not be any other choice in this case.

He headed back to the room, stopping to knock on Kayla's door before returning to his own. He used the coded knock they had arranged, so she knew it was him and opened the door a crack.

"Nice walk?" she said.

"Delightful."

She followed him and he shut the door to his room, hitting both locks.

Kayla dropped into a chair. "What next?"

"I want to find Wexler."

"All right," she said. "I have a friend I can call and get some information."

"They'll be watching any friends you have."

"You mean the friends I have left?"

"They'll be watching, Kayla."

"It's not a friend on the police force."

"Who?"

"She's with the FBI."

Speak of the devil...

Raven said, "You sure?"

"It will work. It will be okay."

Raven looked at her doubtfully. He wasn't so sure. Her eyes told him she wasn't certain either.

He didn't see they had any other choice at the moment.

Chelsea Brandt, candidate for district attorney and Dixon King's favorite, held a campaign rally with modest attendance. She spoke outside San Francisco General Hospital, highlighting two shooting victims brought in overnight, telling the crowd gun crimes would be a major focus of her office, and those who thought San Francisco was their personal shooting gallery would feel the brunt of maximum sentences and no mercy.

She had a lot on her mind as she spoke and hoped the crowd didn't detect it. She didn't need her campaign staff, always close by, noticing either. Things were happening today and no mistake. Her opponent, Stephen Kennedy, also had campaign work going, and though their paths weren't scheduled to cross, plans were in motion to make sure Kennedy suddenly faced obstacles he had no power to walk away from. All he could do was surrender.

He was, though he didn't know it, scheduled to cross paths with Danielle Rawlings.

Being closely connected to the prostitute still bothered Chelsea, and she'd been popping sleeping pills at night to help her doze off, because otherwise she'd lay awake all night. She had no intention of explaining to her husband why sleep eluded her or lie about why. Her husband saw through her more than anybody. It was his superpower. She hated it.

But Wexler vouched for the girl. She'd performed well in the past. She'd do her job again, vanish, and keep her mouth shut.

But what if...

It was the "what if" that bothered Chelsea the most.

Stephen Kennedy, his staff in tow, along with a few report-ers taking pictures, did a "walk and talk" along Market Street. He engaged shoppers and pedestrians, trying to filter out the San Francisco citizens from the tourists and those who only worked in the city and lived outside San Francisco County.

Kennedy's visit to a major shopping hub in the city had a primary purpose.

The previous DA, the late Dan Whitlow, had helped campaign for Proposition 47, which instituted a policy saying shoplifters wouldn't be prosecuted unless they stole merchandise totaling over $950. The dollar amount applied to not only single items, but multiple items; not one attempt at theft, but several. Thieves were walking into stores, stealing items, passing them on to somebody else, and going back to steal more. As long as they didn't hit the $950 limit on any one trip, they walked away.

Storeowners were both furious and powerless to prevent the shoplifting. Many cornered Kennedy to ask him about his feelings on the policy, and he promised he would endorse and campaign for a new proposition to repeal Prop. 47. He heard plenty of stories of people coming in to steal items and brazenly walk out knowing the police wouldn't bother them.

All part of Whitlow's "criminal justice reform" to keep minor offenders out of jail while rehabilitating those already inside.

To the cops, it made no sense. Worn down by so many such

policies from the city and their do-nothing leadership, they had no choice but to accept and follow the rules.

To Kennedy, it was a setup for a tragedy. Somebody was going to get hurt in the process of a theft. Always. Allowing crime to happen didn't save anybody, and only opened the door to more problems, including wrongful death lawsuits against the city. If the government, who had a duty to protect citizens via police, couldn't or wouldn't provide such protection, litigators had the opportunity to bleed the city dry, a city already suffering massive budget deficits. He made the point repeatedly during impromptu engagements, which turned into small speeches.

The applause and enthusiastic reactions from the public encouraged Kennedy as he moved up and down the lengthy street. No wonder he was ahead in the polls. Chelsea Brandt didn't want to change a thing. She was status quo all the way. Another "do nothing" politician looking for a cushy job on public pay.

Kennedy's enthusiasm carried over to a dinner and fundraiser that night, because he had plans for after. Plans with a woman who wasn't the delicious Melissa Doyle or his wife, Brooke.

In between the walk and talk and evening event, Kennedy managed to call Danielle, who had written a big check at his last event and passed him her card "for later". He wanted to speak with her one on one about any issues or concerns she had, and she delightfully agreed to his request. She even suggested he come to her condo in the Rincon Tower.

He laughed. He knew the Rincon well. What she innocently called a "condo" was a "luxury apartment" the Rincon was known for, and residents paid premium condo prices for homes that didn't qualify.

Kennedy couldn't wait. Attendees of the fundraising dinner noted his energy, found it infections, and wrote more checks.

The district attorney's office was all but his.

Kennedy blew off Melissa Doyle because his wife was home. He told Brooke he'd be at the campaign office late going over the schedule for the next few weeks. There was another debate approaching, and he needed to prepare.

Brooke Kennedy didn't argue.

Danielle Rawlings answered the door with a big smile. "Hi!"

She wore a pantsuit too big for her, covering any attribute hinted at on their first meeting. Kennedy stepped through the door and wanted to swim around in her big bright eyes.

"Sorry I'm still in my work clothes," she said. "Busy day today."

"I can wait while you change."

"Sure. Let me get you a drink first."

They had to step down into the living room adjoining the kitchen, and it was worth the step.

The spotless balcony windows looked out on the bay. The twinkling lights of the Bay Bridge, coming on as they did at twilight each evening, were almost mesmerizing.

She caught him staring.

"There's the reason I pay so much rent," Danielle said. "Sometimes I don't even watch TV. I put on Hank Williams, sit out there with a glass of wine, and stare at the lights.

"*'I'm so lonesome I could cry.'*"

"Oh, you're a fan?"

"If it ain't country, I ain't listening."

"Right on!"

"Out of curiosity, what do you pay for rent?"

"About five grand a month for this level."

He had no idea if it was true or if she was trying to make herself sound like a high roller, but it was probably close.

"Too much even for me," Kennedy said.

The furniture impressed him too. She'd stocked the apartment with leather couches and chairs and a glass coffee table that appeared invisible the way it was cut and polished. If it hadn't been for the base, which Danielle said was carved from petrified wood off the Half Moon Bay coast, he wouldn't have realized it was there.

One wall contained her mounted big screen and a stereo rack with CD players, turntable, and cassette deck. She told Kennedy she loved music of all types and not all of it was digital, so she was ready for any format. The CDs and tapes along one side the display, inserted into display racks, were too numerous to count, and Kennedy had other ideas, like what was underneath the pantsuit and how long would it take for him to find out.

Her corner bar wasn't huge but had enough choices for Kennedy to ask for a 7-and-7 which Danielle deftly mixed and watched while Kennedy took his first sip.

"Terrific," he said.

"Just what you need after a long day, right?" She smiled wide. He hadn't noted her large mouth before. Her teeth shined, and when she smiled, the upper portion of her nose crinkled a little.

"You have no idea," he said.

She tilted her head. "What else do you like after work?"

Kennedy drank some more, exhaling with satisfaction. "Well, now that you mention it..."

"No need to be shy." She bit her lower lip again.

He grinned. He wasn't going to dive in too quickly, and his little attempt at innuendo was ill-timed. But wow she looked good. Mostly, she was young. She was younger than both his wife and Melissa Doyle, though only a few years compared with Melissa, he wondered if her age might mean she didn't have as much experience. But who knew? Maybe she'd been with more men than her years indicated.

"Usually a couple of drinks," he said, "is all I need."

"That's it?" She laughed.

"I'm a simple guy with simple tastes."

"Let me top that off for you."

She poured more Seagram's into the glass.

"No 7UP?"

"No, no more 7UP." She stepped closer, looking up at his face, another lip bite. He didn't break her gaze despite the movement of her hands. He didn't see what she was doing, but soon enough he felt massaging fingers at his crotch.

"I want to talk about polls," she said.

"Really?"

"Rising polls."

"I thought I was the only one who made that joke."

"We need to examine these poll numbers right now, Mr. Kennedy." She went for the kiss and he intercepted, the drink forgotten, Kennedy placing the glass on the bar counter before grabbing her and pulling her even closer, feeling the heat of her body through both of their clothes, and the soft pressing of her breasts against his chest.

She kept her hands busy, finally undoing his belt and slacks and before he knew it, he felt a chill on his legs because his slacks had fallen to his ankles but who cares since she was working the poll to a level he wasn't used to feeling even with Melissa Doyle doing the work.

He pulled away. He was breathing heavy, while Danielle Rawlings had not only a glint in her eye but didn't seem to have lost her breath at all.

"Couch or bedroom?" he said.

"There's more room in the bedroom."

She pivoted and started down the hall.

Kennedy hitched up his slacks and followed her.

As Danielle Rawlings finished undressing Kennedy and examined his fit and muscular body, she giggled, feeling his chest and arms, running her fingers through the gray-tinged chest hair, remarking he was in better shape than she'd expected.

"Candidates for office," he said, despite the awkward tent in his boxers, and his black socks, "have to be ready for a long race."

"Nice," she said, and her thumbs snaked through the waistband of Kennedy's shorts and down they want. She shoved him toward the bed. He hesitated. She shoved again, laughing, and he sat on the soft comforter. She put her hands on her hips.

"Just going to sit there? Lie down."

"All right."

He stretched out and put his head on the pillow.

"Those poll numbers are impressive."

He smiled, putting his hands behind his head. "It took a lot of canvassing to get there."

"*Canvassing* is a good word for it."

She started undressing.

Good grief, if this was any easier, I'd be stealing my pay.

But there lay Stephen Kennedy, fully erect and totally at ease, on the bed; he'd fallen right into her trap, and it hadn't taken any real work at all.

Danielle had expected to "force the pace" as she liked to say and meet Kennedy for a second time before inviting him to "her place" in the Rincon. It wasn't her place at all. She certainly wasn't expected to do the deed at her hotel. The condo, provided by Chelsea Brandt's connection, was equipped with the video gear needed to make sure Stephen Kennedy's play time was saved for posterity.

Camera one: behind the mirror on the dresser directly in front of the bed.

Camera two: in the closet, where one side was open to expose her clothes, with a strategic gap for the lens planted in the wall.

Two different angles to make sure nothing was missed.

And with her keeping the lights on, taking her time getting Kennedy out of his suit, the cameras would not only miss nothing, but allow no excuses for poor video quality or lack of light. Kennedy would be on video with no chance to spin his way out of the images she intended to make sure the cameras captured.

She kept up a running narrative while she kicked off her heels.

"You must think I'm horrible."

"Not at all."

She unbuttoned the bulky slacks and pulled down the zipper.

"I don't normally do this."

The slacks fell and she stepped away, her long legs perfectly smooth, her little star tattoo on her right ankle visible if he cared to look, but his eyes weren't there.

"Yes, I wear boring underwear," she said with a laugh. Part of the gag. The leather stuff might have tipped him off she was a working girl. "I like my bottom covered."

"Who doesn't?" he said.

She left the panties on and shrugged out of her suit jacket, the extra-length white blouse puffy in front for concealment, and soon that was gone too, the clothing items ending in a pile at her feet. She grinned at him. His eyes were taking in all of her, head to toe and points in between, and if he noticed her nose, he gave no indication. It was like always. Her imperfections meant little to whichever client she dealt with.

The frustration visible on Kennedy's face amused her too,

but he wouldn't have to wait much longer. She slipped off the bra, put her hands on her hips, and said, "What's the verdict?"

"You forgot something."

"What?" She looked down. "Oh my gosh, right?" She laughed. "See? I told you I don't always do this! I'm such a *noob*." She dropped the panties, kicked them away, and made the pose again. "Now?" She added to the titillation by running her hands under her breasts to give them a squeeze and twisted her nipples to give him a hint of what she might like.

"The hell with your bridge view," he said.

"How much would this view cost?" she said.

If he only knew. . .

"I think you better get over here."

She did, immediately dropping the innocent act, leaving no doubt as to her skill level. They took their time and she even offered a second round, which he didn't refuse. And the cameras captured all.

CHAPTER TWENTY-THREE

Inspector Kayla Blaine scheduled the meeting with her FBI friend across the bay in Berkeley.

Special Agent Cindy Chu found her in the lobby of the Berkeley Marina Hilton, and they found a table in the lobby restaurant for a light lunch.

Sam Raven remained in the background, always somewhere in Kayla's line of sight, watching for danger. She liked having him near and regretted her earlier antagonistic attitude. But who could blame her? He certainly didn't seem to, which she appreciated. He was a man who probably understood what she was going through, and it made her wonder how much violence he actually saw.

It made her feel a little sad.

Cindy Chu quickly brought her back to reality.

"What the hell is going on with your beat?"

Kayla blinked. "What?"

"We're hearing all kinds of rumors," Cindy said. The waitress arrived and they ordered half turkey sandwiches and salads and sweetened iced tea. "Safe house burned to the ground after a hit? Witness dead? *What* witness, Kayla? What's happening? I can see you're *hiding* a bruise. You need more makeup to make it invisible."

"A lot of it I can't talk about," Kayla said, "and never mind the bruise. You can help if you don't mind doing a little digging for me. Unofficially, of course."

"You're asking a favor."

"I am."

"Why not ask through channels?"

"I can't."

Cindy Chu blinked. Kayla didn't break her gaze. As a special agent attached to the Organized Crime Unit, Cindy Chu had seen more of the Bay Area mafia activity than Kayla ever would, and she could sniff out any snow job Kayla attempted to spread. She planned to tell her friend the truth, but only so much. She'd have to understand there were things Kayla simply could not mention.

"Something wrong with the plumbing?"

"It's awful," Kayla said. "We need all-new pipes. The ones we have are leaking like crazy."

"I think I get it."

"That's all I can say."

"I understand."

"How's your family?" Kayla said. As a single woman, she often lived vicariously through her married friends, of which Cindy Chu was one. The chitchat was a stall to wait out the food delivery. She didn't want to be talking real business when the waitress arrived with the order.

They talked about Cindy's family and how her twin daughters were getting ready for their freshman year in high school. Kayla delighted in the news. She'd known the twins since they were babies.

The waitress arrived, and as they ate, Kayla began her spiel.

Cindy leaned forward, shocked at the mention of Leonard Wexler's name.

"You can't be serious."

"I need to know where he is."

"Now *I'm* the one who can't talk," Cindy said. "*Active* investigation. And you have bad plumbing."

"This isn't for the department."

"I don't understand."

"It's personal. It's for me. I was at the safe house when it was hit."

Cindy Chu let out a curse, her food seemingly forgotten. But not for long. Cindy stabbed her fork into the salad and swallowed a few bites before continuing.

"It's my ass if this gets out."

"I may not have an ass," Kayla said, "if I don't take care of this problem."

"How many others are dead besides cops?"

"Two."

"Including your witness?"

"Yes. Both civilians."

"That reporter they fished out of the bay?"

"He's the second one."

They ate some more. The sweetened tea was perfect, and Kayla drank some through her straw while Cindy considered her request further.

"What exactly do you want?" Cindy said.

"An address maybe. Somewhere I can find him. And one of his goons, too. Preferably one with a big gash on the side of his head."

"Francesco Cordova," Cindy said. "He goes by 'Frank'. Whoever hit him gave him a mild concussion and he went to San Francisco General. My people spotted him there. He's been alternating between rest at home and bar across the street from his apartment."

Kayla smiled. She'd have to tell Raven the result of his

gun strike.

"He responsible for your bruise? Or Wexler?"

"Cordova."

Cindy nodded. "You didn't get any of this from me," she said.

"I'm not telling a soul."

Cindy began fishing through her big purse. "And you better not be the next victim." She took out a pen and notepad and set the pad on the table. She started writing.

"I don't intend to be a victim at all," Kayla said.

Cindy didn't look up as she scribbled. "None of us do. But it still happens."

Kayla said she was well aware of that particular fact of life.

Raven followed Kayla to the end of the marina, glancing now and then at the impressive boats, which filled the available slips. He lived on a houseboat in Stockholm, at a private marina not as nice, which also lacked the spectacular view. The end of the marina extended into the bay. Off to one side, the rumble of traffic on the Bay Bridge seemed louder than it should have at the distance they were at; to the right, more tranquil water, and the rest of Berkeley pointing into Richmond.

Kayla stared across the water into the San Francisco skyline in the distance. He stopped beside her.

"Are you all right?" he said.

"I think so," she said. The wind blew her hair into her face. She brushed it away. "Cindy's what I should have been."

"An FBI agent?"

"Married," Kayla said.

"I understand."

She turned to him. "Do you?"

"I *was* married once," Raven said. "A long time ago."

"Is she in the locket?"

"Maybe."

She turned away and didn't say anything more. The chilly wind pushed her hair around some more and she tied it up with a grunt of frustration.

"What did Cindy tell you?" Raven said.

"I have an address for Wexler and the goon you smacked in the head. His name is Francesco Cordova. You gave him a concussion, by the way. She's going to look into some other things too."

"How nice. Where?"

"Wexler has a place near Lombard Street and Cordova lives on Larkin Street."

"Should we get going?"

"It's so quiet here. Even with the bridge."

Raven looked out at the water. A sense of peace came over him, as it always did when he watched the ocean. This portion of the bay was still, yet it had the same effect.

"Let's stay for a while," Raven said.

Peace was hard to find. One had to enjoy when available.

CHAPTER TWENTY-FOUR

"How did the video turn out?" King said.

Wexler, sitting in his car, fiddled with the USB drive in his left hand. "I have no idea. It's on a stick drive. Chelsea says the girl told her it was perfect."

"We have to see it to be sure."

Wexler laughed. "Sure."

"Bring it to the restaurant and we'll look. What about the girl?"

"Chelsea told her to hang out at the hotel for another day or two in case the video isn't good enough."

"All right," King said. "Once we confirm the video, I want the girl taken out. She's been good for us in the past, but this is three jobs now and it's too much."

"No problem."

"Get over here."

Wexler hung up and started the car.

If they were going to engage in breaking and entering, Raven said, he needed tools. They stopped at his room at the Hyatt long enough to grab a set of lock picks from the secret bottom of his trick suitcase.

He unrolled the kit on the dresser to check the picks. Kayla watched him.

"When I worked traffic years ago," she said, "we had a guy who loved picking locks."

"Some people make a hobby out of it."

"He'd stay after his shift when we'd all cleared out and pick the locks on our lockers. Drove us nuts."

Raven smiled as he rolled the kit up and tucked it inside his jacket.

"Then one day," Kayla continued, "somebody took advantage and ripped off a bunch of stuff from the lockers. We all blamed the picker, but he denied it."

"Ever find out who it was?"

She shook her head. "It remains one of the many unsolved cases of the SFPD."

They laughed.

Raven drove the BMW down Sansome Street all the way to the end where it met Lombard, where the one-way street forced a right turn.

Kayla said finding a parking space on the street might require a miracle, but she'd left her Rosary at home. Raven suggested they might have luck on their side and found curbside parking where he stopped the rental and Kayla used her credit card to pay the meter. She set the time for 30 minutes.

They walked along Lombard to the 101 Lombard Condominium complex. She explained most of the buildings on the block belonged to television stations, noting the many aerials on the roofs of four buildings. Cops could count on the TV people making trouble at two or three bars up the block most of them frequented after their shifts.

"And here I thought people on TV were the cream of the crop," Raven remarked.

Wexler's condo complex seemed out of place, smack between two larger business complexes, the front facing the street. It was as if a stubborn landlord wanted to use the building for housing instead of business, and damn what anybody else wanted to do.

The office buildings cast a chilly shadow over the street.

The three levels of the mostly red brick condo building had windows marking each floor. The small size told Raven there weren't many units, and their odds improved with the knowledge. With fewer people home, and Wexler was certainly on the road, their unlawful entry might go unnoticed. Unless a busybody at one of the neighboring buildings happened to be looking out the window and spying on their arrival.

A chance worth taking.

He hustled up a flight of steps to the glass entry doors, stepping into the lobby. On the other end, more glass doors led to the pool in back of the building. There was no reception desk, but a doorway near the pool entrance was marked OFFICE. Based on the size of the building, he speculated three employees, max.

The elevator quietly brought them to the third floor. Wexler's condo faced the rear, overlooking the pool. The condo doors were plain white while the hallway walls were light beige, the carpet showing little signs of wear.

At the door, Raven stood to one side, Kayla the other, and Raven knocked. No answer. Raven waited a few moments and pressed the doorbell. Still no answer.

Kayla said, "Let's kick it in."

"Not sporting, my dear," Raven said. Picklocks in hand, he knelt before the doorknob and deadbolt and went to work.

"What about an alarm?" she said.

Raven, using his tools, focused on the locks. "I'm sure he has one."

"It will be loud."

"It won't be one programmed to call police."

"You think?"

"It will probably call two car-loads' worth of King's goons."

"Why two?"

"It's a round number."

Kayla opened her jacket and drew her pistol.

The doorknob lock popped, and Raven gave it a twist. It turned all the way. Now for the deadbolt...

When Raven pushed the door open, no alarms sounded.

"Must be a silent alarm," he said. "Come on."

Kayla kept her pistol out while she and Raven entered the front room, noting how clean it was, the fine furniture. It seemed as if Wexler spent most of his time chasing specks of dust and making sure one could eat off the floor. She wanted to see the bathroom and find out if his obsession extended to that part of the house.

"Something's not right," she said.

"I know, he has no television."

"Special kind of freak, huh?"

"Or the smartest man on the planet."

The white walls were bare of any decoration, including the ubiquitous mounted flat screen. There weren't even bare spots to suggest something had once been displayed on a wall. Doing so probably ruined Wexler's sense of orderliness.

Raven wasn't terribly surprised. He'd known many people like Wexler, specialists in violent work, who were clean freaks, because it gave them a sense of control over their personal environment when their work environments were very dirty. After snapping necks and breaking balls all day, Leonard Wexler was a man who liked to return to a domicile promoting calmness and serenity. As usual in cases like this, Raven wondered what such people could do if they turned their obsessive energy into something productive. The world needed fewer killers; actually, didn't need them at all. If no killers existed in the world, Raven might have become something productive as well.

Perhaps a dentist. Maybe an electrician.

The maybes of his life often passed through his thoughts in quiet moments.

Raven checked the two bedrooms and single bathroom and found all empty, all immaculate, and Kayla didn't believe him about the bathroom, so she went to look for herself. She emerged saying, "I didn't think a man existed who could clean like this."

Kayla stayed in the living room while Raven moved into the kitchen, his shoes squeaking on the floor. Clean counters, spotless stove. A set of cookbooks near the stove and they had been well read indeed. Raven picked up one book, noting the Post-It marks Wexler had left on certain pages. He preferred complex dishes, rich foods, a lot of pasta and chicken. Raven returned the cookbook to its place.

He found Post-It notes in a small container on the counter along with a pen, scribbled a quick note, and smacked it onto the wall in front of the couch. Wexler might not have a television, but he'd for sure see the note when he finally took a load off on the couch.

"What did you write?"

"'Love and Kisses, Sam Raven'. Let's get out of here."

"I want to kick something over, throw toilet paper around, something."

"No, dear, let's go before we wear out our welcome."

As they stepped into the hall, Raven pulled the door shut.

"Going to lock it?"

"No," Raven said. "It will add to the surprise."

They exited the way they'd arrived.

The quiet elevator deposited them into the lobby. Out the glass doors to the steps. . .

A black Audi left a two-inch patch of rubber on the street as the car screeched to a stop in the street. Other drivers behind the Audi let their horns do the talking until four men piled out carrying submachine guns. Then the drivers either sped around the Audi, briefly crossing into the opposing lane, or made hasty U-turns.

Kayla said, "You were right about our welcome!"

Raven shoved Kayla to the right, toward two rectangular planters with hedges growing in the enclosed dirt. "Down!"

The first two salvos tore through the hedges, Raven pressing his body onto Kayla's, bullets smacking the wall behind them, chunks of stucco raining down as the slugs whined off. One ricochet exploded on the concrete beside Raven's right elbow.

Raven shouted for her to stay flat as the firing ceased and shuffling feet scraped their way up the steps. Yelling from inside drew a second of his attention as a woman stuck her head out of the half-open OFFICE door. She was smart enough to slam the door shut.

Half the neighborhood would be calling 911 so Raven had to work fast.

He knew he had no choice but to return fire. This wasn't a situation where he could lure the attackers to another location. He rose into a squat, turning his back to Kayla as he drew the Nighthawk Custom, and fired once around the side of the hedge. The big .45 thundered, a hollow-point slug punching through the gunner in the lead, stopping him cold. He tumbled down the steps, leaving a trail of blood, stopping in a sprawl on the sidewalk where the red pool grew beneath him. His buddies scrambled.

Two made for the planters opposite Raven, not bothering to fire, and the Nighthawk Talon spoke again. One man dropped, the other making cover, but not clearing the hedge fast enough. Raven saw enough of him through the greenery to fire another round and rip a hole into his back.

The third gunner ran to the Audi. Raven rose, extended his pistol, but held his fire as the man jumped behind the wheel and took off. Gawkers had gathered across the street, and while they'd been smart enough to get behind cover, each one had their heads high enough to see the action. A miss might have hit one. Raven watched the Audi speed to the next corner and turn onto Battery Street, the tires smoking, the lingering cloud fading fast.

He hauled Kayla to her feet. She was pale, shaking. She had enough wits about her to raise her badge and shout she was with the SFPD and for somebody to call 911. Raven laughed—somebody had done so already, no doubt. Raven hustled her across the street to the BMW, shoving her in, sliding across the hood to his side. He accelerated toward the Embarcadero one block ahead.

Kayla sat frozen, her still looking pale.

"Are you hit?" Raven said.

She didn't reply.

He raised his voice. "Kayla, have you been shot?"

She frantically felt around her body, behind her back. "No."

"What's wrong?"

"That was too close. Too close. I can't keep *doing* this!"

She put her hands to her face and let out an anguished cry. The stress and anxiety of the last several days was now bubbling to the surface. He'd expected the reaction, but the delay surprised him. He'd have thought she'd crack much sooner. Inspector Kayla Blaine was a tough lady, and her tolerance for stress was a credit to her. The problem was each person, no matter what, had a limit, and Inspector Kayla Blaine had apparently reached her limit.

He needed another approach to the problem. Going into the heart of the enemy camp wasn't going to work. He'd had a sound plan before and needed to stick with it.

They also needed another hideout. Too many witnesses had seen the BMW, and their faces. While witnesses might differ on physical descriptions, they'd know the BMW, and the cops would look for the car before looking for them. Time to ditch the car for another and leave the hotel for a second sanctuary. Raven had an idea where.

Luckily, it was a short trip to the Hyatt, and they reached Raven's room without anybody else trying to kill them.

CHAPTER TWENTY-FIVE

She sat on the bed with her shoulders slumped as Raven started packing.

"Where are we going?"

"New hideout. I figure Marin is a good place."

She watched him blankly as he loaded his suitcase.

"Better get your stuff together, Kayla."

She didn't move.

"That was too close," she repeated once again.

"Too close, or the last straw?"

"Yes."

Raven zipped his suitcase closed. He went to her, bent down, and put his hands on her shoulders. "It's all right. I'm not going anywhere."

"What do I do if something happens to you?"

Raven blinked.

"I can't do this on my own."

"I'm here now."

"But what if you *aren't*? Look, isn't there somebody you can call for help?"

Raven let go of her and stood. "I'm alone. I have friends I could call, sure, but they won't get here in time. We don't have the time to wait for them. It's only us, Kayla."

"What kind of *life* do you *actually* lead, Sam?"

"The one I chose. For better or worse."

She left the bed and made a sharp turn for the door. Raven moved out of her way. "I need to think about this."

"Kayla."

Halfway to the door, she stopped and turned to face him. Her hair looked jumbled from the fight, and she pushed it out of her face. Some color had returned, but there was no doubt her spirit had taken a beating, and she needed time to recover. They still had a long way to go.

"You're tough," he said, "and I admire you've been able to get this far without cracking."

"I think I cracked a second ago."

"No. It's a natural reaction, but you haven't cracked. There won't be any question when you do."

He hoped the words set her mind at ease, if only a little.

"What you need to do," he continued, "is reach down deep for more strength. One more tank of gas. You can do it, Kayla. We're almost done."

"We haven't accomplished *anything*!"

"As soon as I find out who King's candidate is—"

"You sound a lot like somebody saying, 'When I win the lottery.'"

"We can get through this together." He approached her. "We can."

She lowered her face and turned away from his gaze. He reached for her shoulders again. "Kayla—"

Her arms were around his neck and her lips on his. Raven was too startled to pull back, so he gave in. Her lips were warm, her body hot against his, and she squeezed him tightly, a drowning woman looking for anything to grab ahold of and he simply happened to be there.

She seemed fragile in his arms. Her body was too lean and muscular to have anything to grab onto, so all he felt were bones. Raven broke the kiss and gave her a gentle push.

He said, "We can't."

Her face flushed red and she hurried out of the room. The bathroom door swung shut behind her with a crack of finality.

Raven let out a breath and sat down on the bed. He had priorities and needed to focus on them. He needed to keep her safe long enough to end the alliance between Dixon King and Abelard Joulbert. That was the mission. The mission came first. Always.

He wasn't there to fall in love.

Kayla turned on the faucet and splashed water on her face once, twice. She roughly dried her skin with a washcloth, smearing her makeup onto the white cloth, and when she looked at her face in the mirror, the bruise was more paramount than after the makeup coverage, and it startled her.

Oh, God, what is happening...

She lowered the toilet lid and sat down, staring at the floor. She felt confused, angry, once again out of control. What was she thinking kissing Raven? She understood a little of what was happening. She had a savior complex. Raven "the Rock". Unshakable. Sure-footed. Knew what to do. He was a man comfortable with conflict, but not comfortable with the death within the conflict. It made him vulnerable, gave him a soft side he didn't necessarily show.

But he was right. They couldn't forge any other connection than the one they had on the surface. He was there to do a job; so was she. He could leave when his job was done, but Kayla had to live with the results. She had a life to rebuild. There was no room for a romantic entanglement leading only to a dead end.

She needed to stay focused on the task, not muddy the waters by being sentimental.

Along with the flurry of thoughts in her mind, she also wanted to go home.

To Connecticut. Her parents were there, the comfort of family waiting to re-embrace her, and all she had to do was get on a plane. She didn't even need to call. She could show up at the door unannounced and they wouldn't ask any questions until she finally fell apart. She wanted to tell her father he had been right all this time, joining the cops was a mistake, and ask for help trying to correct the mistake.

But it wasn't the answer. Running was never the answer.

Her life had always been orderly and disciplined and there was no need to step out of her pattern. Yeah, some guys with automatic weapons had tried to kill her multiple times. Anybody would freak out, but she had to take a measure of control if they were going to finish the race. Her job was to *not* freak out but save the anger and rage for the enemy when she finally had them in her sights. *Stay in the pattern. It's kept you alive and will continue to do so.*

She left the bathroom to pack her bag and rejoin Raven.

For a moment they stared at each other.

He said, "I thought—"

"What?"

"There's an AirBNB in Marin we can use."

"Does the owner live at the house?"

"No. It will only be us. It's close enough to the city for us to get back quickly. It's not connected to you in any way. We have to change cars, but that won't take long."

"Okay."

"Are you all set?"

She showed him her tote bag and purse.

"We need to go right now."

Raven grabbed his suitcase and held the door for her. She exited into the hallway and the door shut behind them.

They walked to the elevator. Raven wanted to say more, but the words were frozen in his mind. He wanted to pretend the kiss hadn't happened, but he also knew a line had been crossed.

Her question nagged at him.

"What kind of life *do you* actually *lead, Sam?"*

The life he chose.

Or was it the one chosen for him?

Either way it was a lonely life.

And he often felt like a drowning victim, too.

CHAPTER TWENTY-SIX

The owner of the AirBNB met them at the house. She was a recent widow who had decided to use her and her husband's former home as a rental while she moved to an apartment. Raven said he understood. It's hard to stay in a home full of memories. Good ones weren't enough to remain; the bad memories, the pain of loss, overruled anything pleasant one might remember.

She gave them a tour and handed over the keys, told them to contact her with any issues, and departed. Raven and Kayla brought from the car two bags of groceries and settled into the house.

It was a small one-story home, with an equally small back yard, but a large porch. The owner had filled the yard with some chairs and a bright garden. The kitchen counter was full of collector plate displays and other odds and ends. Working space on the counter was at a premium. But there were two bedrooms and a comfortable living room, so the new hideout sufficed. Raven didn't expect they would be staying long. Another two days, max. It was all the time they had before the election.

After storing the groceries in the refrigerator and pantry,

Raven found Kayla sitting on the couch. She stared out the still-curtained front window at the street.

Similar houses to theirs sat across the street, cars lining the curb from one end to the other. Three children rode by on bicycles, shouting at each other as they pedaled. It all seemed so normal, yet they were part of a totally different reality than Raven and her occupied. For now.

He sat across from her.

"We can hang out here till night," he said. "Then it's time to go talk to the candidates."

"I'm going to stay."

"Are you sure?"

"I won't go anywhere."

"Not what I meant."

"I'll be fine. I need to be alone for a while."

"Understandable."

"This place is safe enough and the neighborhood looks quiet. I have my gun."

Raven stood up. "Come with me."

She followed him down a short hallway to the bedroom he'd picked, a small room with bright wallpaper and more gaudy decorations.

He unbolted the X-ray proof bottom of his suitcase and assembled the M4 Commando. He held the weapon out for her. "Do you know how to use this?"

She took it, giving the short carbine a quick examination. "Looks like an M4."

"It is an M4, but with a shorter barrel."

"I'm checked out on the M4, yeah."

He took the gun from her and screwed on the custom suppressor. "That'll keep it quiet."

"Tell the other guys."

He propped the M4 in a corner. "Only if there's an emergency. It would be a shame to shoot up all the crap in this house."

Neither laughed, though Raven had hoped she would. She looked better than when they left the Hyatt but was still wound too tightly. A good laugh might have loosened her up. Or he needed a better joke. He'd try again later. He looked at her quietly instead. She stood between him and the doorway.

"You okay?" he said.

"I want my life back, Sam."

"You'll have it back."

She nodded.

"Well," he said, "why don't we fix something to eat?"

"Okay."

They went to the kitchen where she insisted on doing most of the cooking but asked Raven to chop the vegetables.

In his office at Martha's Restaurant, Dixon King looked up as Leonard Wexler's bulk filled the doorway.

King removed his glasses and set aside paperwork. "What took you so long? Got the video?"

"I have the damn video, Dixon. Hear about my condo?"

"Uh-huh."

"That bastard Raven left me a note."

King laughed. "A what?"

"A note. A Post-It on my wall."

"What did it say?"

"'Love and kisses'."

King let out another laugh, a deep one. The sound filled the hallway.

"It's not funny, Dixon."

King wiped his eyes. "No, it isn't, but it is at the same time."

Wexler ducked his head to enter the office and dropped into the chair in front of King's desk.

"They aren't playing defense anymore," the big man said.

"Apparently not."

"The problem is getting worse, and we're running out of time."

"You're right," King said. "I heard from Dresnik. He thinks Blaine is talking to an FBI agent friend of hers."

"He give you a name?"

"Cindy Chu."

"What makes him think they're talking?"

"Increased chatter from agents in the city," King said. "They're stirred up."

"We've done enough to stir them up. Of course, they're looking into things."

"It's more than he'd expect. They're talking about Whitlow and Kline, and he doesn't like it. Those cases are none of their business, but now they're trying to make a connection *with* their business."

Wexler blinked and waited.

"We don't have any friends in the bureau office, Leo."

"I'm well aware, Dixon."

"Federal heat could ruin us."

"I was about to say so."

"Chu is a local." King handed Wexler a piece of paper with an address written on it. "I suggest you stick with her and see where she takes us. She and Blaine will meet again. If they do, don't touch the Fed, but make sure you get Blaine."

Wexler folded the paper and put it in a pocket.

"Let's see the USB drive."

Wexler fished the stick drive from a pocket and tossed it to King, who caught it. King opened a drawer and pulled out a small laptop, which quickly booted, and he inserted the drive into a USB port.

Two files representing the views from two cameras. King turned the screen so Wexler could see and clicked the first file. The bed faced the camera. Kennedy occupied the bed in an obvious state of excitement. Danielle Rawlings stood a little out of the frame, and took her time removing her clothes. There was no sound.

Danielle Rawlings climbed onto the bed and did what she was hired to do.

The second video showed a better view from the side. Kennedy liked changing positions, so his face was always front and center.

King closed the laptop lid. "Good. I'll keep it at the house."

Wexler laughed and shook his head. "It's like we're sneaking a look at your pops' dirty movies all over again."

King smiled at the memory. His old man had no idea how easy it had been to find the stash. "I gotta finish this," King said, gesturing to the paperwork. "You go find the FBI lady. And tell the guys to hit the girl in the video when they get a chance."

"Done," Wexler said.

Raven picked up Stephen Kennedy's trail in the evening.

Commuter traffic across the Golden Gate Bridge delayed his arrival at one of Kennedy's speaking engagements, but he caught most of the man's speech and the Q&A.

When Kennedy left the event, Raven trailed behind him in the new rental car, a Dodge Challenger this time. The Challenger lacked leather seats, but the cloth buckets were comfortable enough.

Kennedy drove to a condominium building and parked in the basement garage. Raven found street parking and watched the front door, thinking of his next move. Another car pulled into a curbside spot, and a woman stepped out of the vehicle. She looked both ways before hurrying across the street. She was dressed for business but wore tennis shoes. Raven bet her heels remained in the car.

Raven watched the lithe brunette enter and pressed his lips together in thought. He recognized the woman as one of Kennedy's entourage, one who seemed to have his ear more than the others. Advisor? Whoever she was, she was meeting Kennedy where he was alone. He knew from previous research Kennedy did not live in a condominium, but a house in Daly City. His information was based on newspaper reports. Was this a location hidden from his wife? Or had he relocated to remain in SF for campaign work?

Raven left the car and crossed the street. The basement garage had a door at the sidewalk, securely locked. Raven hung around looking at his cell phone, ignoring passersby. When a couple exited the street door, pushing it wide open, they walked on without looking back. Raven grabbed the door before it closed, slipped inside, and let it close behind him. He followed a well-lit flight of stairs to another door, not locked, and stepped into the garage.

One underground garage is the same as another. Cold concrete, parked vehicles, a fluorescent light on the fritz and blinking. The light's ticking sound the only noise within other than street sounds.

He found Kennedy's car and found a dark corner to hide in while keeping the car in view.

He had no idea how long he'd have to wait, but he figured it wouldn't be too long before Kennedy emerged to drive home.

Raven's phone rang.

CHAPTER TWENTY-SEVEN

"Hello, Oscar."

"Why are you whispering?"

"Why do you think?"

Oscar Morey laughed on the other end of the line. "I get it. Ready for some information?"

"What do you have?"

"Rap sheet and photo of Tyrone Biggins, like you asked. It includes a current picture, so you'll know him when you see him."

"Send it to my phone."

"Done."

"Can you check something else?"

"Hit me."

Raven gave him the address of the condo building and said, "Tell me if this matches the address of Stephen Kennedy."

"Hang on."

Morey stayed on the line and Raven heard him tapping a keyboard in the background, calling out to somebody else, and presently returning.

"He has a house in Daly City and ten years left on the mortgage. The condo is registered to his law firm."

"I thought so."

"What's he doing at the condo?"

"Something naughty." A beep sounded in Raven's ear. He consulted the bright screen. A notice of a downloaded file being ready to view displayed.

"Got the file, thank you."

"Anytime."

Melissa Doyle moaned in delight, on her hands and knees, her rear end up, Kennedy behind her with his hands on her hips, thrusting hard.

She urged him on. Harder. Deeper. *Faster.* Kennedy tried to accommodate her, and she bucked against him to help, but he had to laugh. As nice as Danielle Rawlings had been, she couldn't beat Melissa Doyle.

She climaxed first and collapsed, Kennedy pulling out to drop next to her. Panting, their bodies sweaty, she remained on her belly, head on the pillow, her hair in a crazy pattern.

"Well?" she said.

"Wish I could stay longer."

"How long till your wife calls?"

"She won't." Kennedy rolled off the bed and jumped into the shower for two minutes. When he emerged, drying off, Melissa Doyle remained on the bed. It was tough to look at her body and especially her plump rear end and not want to stay longer.

She rolled onto his side to watch him get dressed.

"Not much longer till the election," she said.

"Long enough."

She made more room on the bed so he could sit and tie his shoes. He stood up and smacked her behind. She laughed.

"Down payment on next time."

"Sure," she said.

He left the condo. She had a key to lock up and knew the alarm code. He didn't have to worry about her.

The elevator took him to the garage, and he found his car where he left it. As he clicked the remote opening, he sensed movement behind him, feet shuffling. Before he could turn, something hard pressed into his spine.

"Good evening, Mr. Kennedy."

The man stiffened as Raven pressed the barrel of the Nighthawk Custom into his back.

His voice shook as he spoke. "What do you want?"

"Hands on the car, Stephen."

Kennedy complied, gripping the roof of his car with his hands spread out.

"What do you *want*?" he repeated.

"What are the odds you and your campaign adviser live in the same building?"

"So?"

"You live in Daly City, Stephen."

"Tell me what you *want*!"

"Answers to questions. Are you going to be a good boy and tell me what I want to know?"

"Ask me anything!"

"Are you working for Dixon King?"

Kennedy jerked his head around to try and see over his shoulder. "No!"

"Yet you know who he is."

"*Everybody* knows who he is."

"Everybody in the circle of corruption, you mean?"

"I was *told* about him, okay? Some cops gave me a briefing one day, said to watch out for him and his crew."

"Uh-huh. You're trying to keep up your boy scout image, right?"

"I'm not like the rest of them!"

Raven laughed. "You're a politician for sure, Stephen. You people can never resist your talking points, or not start to give a speech."

"Is there a *point* to all this?"

"It's an easy one. The mob wouldn't exactly tolerate their candidate fooling around on his wife. It poses huge risks. That's the only reason I believe you."

"It's not what you think!"

"What isn't?"

"My...fooling around."

"You're not?"

"I *am!* But only because...my wife and I..."

"Oh, problems at home? What happens when she finds out about your affairs? She'll scream and you'll be in divorce court and an unreliable source of protection for Dixon King."

"But that means—"

"Tell me."

"Are you suggesting *Chelsea* is on the take?"

"You're learning, Stephen. Think about it. Family woman, reputation in the city, beautiful, so she gets a pass on a lot of things to begin with. The public is never rude to pretty people, but if you have a few blemishes, it's another story. Am I right?"

"Hey," Kennedy said, "how about you take the gun out of my back and clarify the lesson a little more?"

Raven considered the request. Kennedy's body still shook, his hands locked on the roof of the car. He wasn't a fighter. He probably had no energy to fight with after his romp upstairs.

Raven said, "Okay," and took the gun away.

Kennedy turned to face him.

CHAPTER TWENTY-EIGHT

Raven laughed. "You're still sweating, Mr. Kennedy."

"This is different." Kennedy leaned against his car but had to work to keep his legs from buckling. Raven figured they felt like Jello.

"Who is the woman upstairs?"

"Melissa Doyle. My campaign advisor."

"She the only one you're stepping out with?"

"Yes. Well, no. *Mostly.*"

"Who else? Interns?"

"No, no, not *interns*, give me *some* credit."

"Who?" Raven said. "Who else are you screwing and which one of them might have compromised you?"

Kennedy frowned. "What are you talking about?"

"If King knows this is a weakness, he'll want to exploit it."

"So you're saying—"

"Who *else?* It's not a hard question."

Kennedy gasped, dropped his head a bit. "I have a card."

Raven let him reach into his jacket. He pulled out a business card with some of the edges folded. Raven took the card in his left hand. He still held the Nighthawk pistol in his right, letting the gun rest against his leg.

"Danielle Rawlings? An app specialist? How many apps do we need that there are so many specialists?"

"She showed up at a fundraiser, and, well...you know."

"I get the idea." Raven put the card in his back pocket. "Anything suspicious about her?"

"It was only a lay, man."

"All right. How often do other *lays* make themselves available to you?"

"You mean—"

"How many *come* on to you, Mr. Kennedy. How hard do you have to work?"

He laughed. "Harder than you think. But this one—"

"She was younger."

"A little, yeah. She started it."

"Haven't heard that one in a long time." Raven put his gun away. "Her place or here at the condo?"

"Her place."

"Where?"

"Rincon Tower." He gave Raven the apartment number.

"How often do you do this at the woman's place, Mr. Kennedy?"

"Only the one time."

"And that's how they got you. Probably on video. They're going to use it to force you out of the race."

"I'm ahead in the polls!"

"There you go again, Mr. Politician. You'll be dead last if the video comes out. Rumors don't often destroy a man and the public will ignore a rumor, but give them hard evidence, a video of you with a woman not your wife, and they'll turn on you so fast you'll wish you'd never been born. They'll spring it in the next twenty-four hours, before the vote. The video will also ruin your marriage and put your law firm at risk. You at least care about one of those things, right?"

Kennedy's reply choked in his throat. He looked sick.

"I care about them both," he managed.

"Sounds like you have some repair work to do at the house."

He nodded.

"Go home, Mr. Kennedy. And I suggest you knock off this crap. You're in danger enough as it is."

"I am?"

"Been watching the news lately?"

"Um...no."

Raven started for the exit.

"Hey!"

He turned. "What?"

"Um...nothing, I guess. Never mind."

"Go home."

Raven resumed his stride to the street exit. Kennedy probably wanted to ask if he'd find the compromising material and bring it to him. Raven laughed. Sure. Kennedy was reckless, not evil. His type could be cured.

The type Dixon King represented?

The only cure was a bullet through the head, or a toss off a roof.

Kayla Blaine had no intention of breaking her word to Raven. They fixed a small meal of seasoned chicken and steamed vegetables and rice. He ate and left before the sun went down. She was going to stay put at the AirBNB.

She put the television on to the Food Network to veg out on a *Chopped* marathon. It was a show she often put on when she only wanted extra noise in her apartment to make it feel less empty. She hoped it did the same trick at the hideout.

She ran her clothes through the washer and dryer. The house came equipped with an ironing board so she could at least get the wrinkles out and hang up the clothes instead of living out of her tote bag.

The alone time was working wonders, exactly as she had wanted. The fact she could pause and do something as simple as iron her clothes proved to be incredible therapy.

Her phone rang.

She muted *Chopped* while sitting on the couch and glanced at the display. It was Cindy Chu calling. She answered.

"I have something for you," Cindy said.

"Tell me."

"It's a file. Can we meet?"

"You're giving me a file?"

"Not officially. How about it?"

Kayla's mind raced. She didn't want Cindy coming to the AirBNB. She also didn't want to leave.

"I'm in Marin," she said.

"Where?"

"I can't say."

"Pick somewhere and we'll talk there."

Kayla gave her the name of a coffee shop she'd seen on the way to the new hideout, and Cindy agreed to meet her in an hour.

Kayla ended the call.

Great. Now she was breaking her word to Raven. But if Cindy had information to help bring an end to Dixon King, she knew Raven would want the details.

Too bad the M4 Commando didn't fit in her purse.

Raven called Oscar Morey as he drove.

"What now?"

"Check an address," Raven said.

"You think I work for you fulltime?"

"You've never told me no yet."

"And I'm not telling you *no* this time, either. I'm getting soft in my old age, Sam. What is it?"

Raven repeated the Rincon Tower apartment address and waited while Oscar did his research.

"What name are you looking for?" Oscar said.

"Danielle Rawlings. Should be on the lease."

"It's not."

"Who is on the lease?"

"The bills go to a place called Martha's Restaurant on Eddy Street. The name on the lease is somebody named William Jones."

Raven laughed. "Who owns the restaurant?"

"Hang on."

More typing in the background. Raven waited in traffic, the stop light ahead only allowing a few cars through before changing again. Cross-traffic seemed to have much more time to flow than his side. The Charger, with its burbling exhaust, wasn't as quiet as the BMW had been. He didn't want to crack the windows because too much marijuana smoke hung in the air.

"Mr. John J. Jones owns the restaurant," Oscar Morey said, "but the cops have it flagged for special attention. It's probably a front for King. If you want, I can cross check with the FBI and see what they have."

"Later. I'm not going to go blow up the place based on suspicion," Raven said. "Thanks, Oscar."

Raven hung up and inched forward, closer to the light. Maybe on the next cycle he'd make it through. He made another call and waited some more.

CHAPTER TWENTY-NINE

Rosie's Coffee sat in the middle of a shopping center. Kayla had no car, so she phoned for an Uber. The driver promptly picked her up. In the back seat, she sat with her .40 caliber SIG Sauer P229 snug under her jacket. Her badge, clipped to her belt, was available in case she needed to use the gun. She thought of the M4 Commando left behind at the house. She'd have been more comfortable carrying both weapons but had no way to hide the carbine in her purse. Such weapons had their drawbacks.

The trip took less than five minutes.

The shopping center parking lot was full, and the Uber driver dropped her at the door to the coffee shop. Kayla entered and looked around. All the tables looked full, the line to the counter about ten deep but then Cindy Chu waved her over from where she sat.

Cindy pushed a coffee to Kayla as she sat down. The chair wobbled; one leg was shorter than the others. Kayla leaned forward to stop the wobble. Kayla took an appreciative sip.

"What do you have?" Kayla said.

"You didn't get this from me," Cindy said. She pulled a manila envelope from her purse. It wasn't bulging with contents, but thick enough to tell Kayla there was plenty of information within.

"Data on Dixon King's holdings," Cindy said. "We know he's stockpiling guns for something, and they're crated at several warehouses. Some of his other places are in here, too, the front companies, the gambling spots, and his place here in Marin, near the bridge."

"He's here? In *Marin?*"

"Big house. Cost him over twenty million."

Kayla took the envelope and put it in her purse.

"Destroy it when you're done," Cindy said. "It's copies of stuff I shouldn't have taken out of the building."

"Why are you doing this?"

"To help you."

"There's more to it, Cindy."

Cindy Chu drank some coffee. "Let's say the Bureau is aware of your friend, okay?"

"My friend?"

"Raven."

"And what interest does the Bureau have in Sam Raven?"

"None, but he's not unknown to us. Come on, Kayla. We saw him in Berkeley when we met the first time."

"We?"

"I didn't go alone."

Anger flared in Kayla's gut, but she kept her mouth shut. As betrayals went, it was a small one. If the FBI wasn't after Sam Raven's head, she assumed, they knew more about him than she did. They wanted to use him for their own ends. She wondered what he'd think.

"I'm sorry," Cindy Chu said. "I didn't mean anything bad."

"It's fine."

"Good luck, Kayla." Cindy slid off the seat and exited the coffee shop, leaving Kayla alone among the other patrons.

They were enjoying their evening while she fought for her life.

And if she wanted her life back, as she'd told Raven, she hoped the information Cindy provided would hasten the achievement of her goal.

She left the table after a few minutes, long enough for Cindy to get on the road, and took the coffee with her. Raven wouldn't begrudge her a quick coffee run if he saw the cup, right? They'd selected Marin because it was safer than San Francisco, hadn't they?

She called for another Uber ride to return to the AirBNB. Five-minute wait. She watched the graphic on her phone showing the driver's progress. When he was turning into the shopping center, Kayla pushed through the door to wait near the entrance. She wanted to remain close to the windows in plenty of light. Small security measure, but it might help.

She couldn't help but feel nervous, but she kept up a danger scan to make sure her trail was clear. There were too many people around for even the dumbest bad guys to try anything. She was being paranoid, yeah. There actually *were* people out to get her.

The door opened behind her. As she turned, she gasped. The big man exiting wasn't unfamiliar. A hulking six feet, dressed in black. The last time she'd seen his face was at the county jail when she and Dresnik had attempted to speak with the late Charlie Kline.

The man grabbed her arm and jammed a pistol into her side.

"Hello, Inspector Blaine," Leonard Wexler said. "We've been waiting for this moment for too long."

Kayla froze as she stared into the big man's face. She wanted to scream, but the cry felt lodged in her throat. She couldn't get it out.

"Scream and you're dead."

She swallowed and nodded.

"We're going for a short ride, Inspector. It won't take long."

So much for safety. So much for being careful. It was all going to end, and Raven would never know what happened.

A black van pulled up, the side door sliding open. The man who opened the door cradled a submachine gun and made room to let Kayla and Wexler enter. She didn't try to fight. The odds were against her. Her small security precautions had been for naught. She was dealing with bad guys who knew the same tricks and worked smarter to get around them.

When the van door slid closed again, she was trapped in the dark interior.

CHAPTER THIRTY

The woman said, "Who is this?"

Raven spoke into his phone as he drove. "We have a mutual friend. We have another job for you."

"What happened to Chelsea?"

Bingo.

"My name is Sam. I'm your contact now. Chelsea's out of it."

"Okay."

"I need to see you. I have the man's picture and instructions. It's a different guy than Kennedy."

The woman sighed. "All right. I was only supposed to stay if we needed another run at Kennedy. My flight back to Vegas is tomorrow morning. This needs to be quick." She added, "A quick in-and-out!" and laughed.

"It won't take long. You'll be paid again. Same fee."

"Where are you?"

"Stuck in traffic. Where are you?"

"Chelsea didn't tell you?"

"All I have is your number, Danielle."

"All right, fine. Marriott Hotel, 4th Street, room 625."

"I'll be there as fast as I can."

Raven ended the call and made a left to pick up 4th Street off Market. He'd been lucky. They'd kept the woman in town instead of sending her home straight away. The fact she was imported from out of state amused him. Whoever she was, her particular skill wasn't one they found with any locals. They didn't call her for anything as simple as giving Whitlow his overdose.

Raven had all he needed. Danielle had conducted the video-taping of Stephen Kennedy, following instructions by Chelsea Brandt, who was setting the plan in motion on behalf of Dixon King. Chelsea doing the dirty work herself must have been a hoot. King was digging a deeper hole for her so she'd remain loyal and do what she was told, and hold the conspiracy over her head if she tried to break away.

When you make a deal with the devil and all that, Raven thought. Some people simply had to learn the hard way.

Raven found the hotel and made his way around a crowded block to the Mission Street entrance of the one-way garage. It was a slow drive. Traffic wasn't the only delay. Pedestrians, packed on the sidewalk, made street driving more difficult by ignoring crosswalks. It was like driving through a human obstacle course. Brake lights flared often.

He let a valet park his car and entered the building. The wide lobby, with a sports bar adjacent to the registration desk, was full of guests. An escalator led to an upper level five-star restaurant. On any other occasion, Raven imagined having a nice evening there, with a nightcap at the lounge at the top of the hotel. The lobby notices promised a panoramic view of the city.

But not tonight.

Raven took the elevator to the sixth floor. He found room 625 and knocked. The woman who answered and half her face around the door.

"I'm Sam."

She opened all the way to let him in. She was dressed casually in jeans and a Tee-shirt, the jeans ripped above the knee. Her dark hair dangled in wild strands.

"Hurry up," she said. He pushed the door shut behind him.

"Where's your stuff?" she said, muting the television and dropping the remote on the bed.

"No stuff, no job."

She looked nervous. "What do you want?"

"For you to get out of town. Not tomorrow, but right now."

"I don't understand."

"Danielle, they aren't going to simply let you leave San Francisco. You are part of something the people who hired you are willing to kill for, and several people have already died. You're next."

"That's crazy. I've done these jobs for so-and-so three times now."

"You have no idea who hired you?"

"Chelsea Brandt made the deal. She called using the same line you did. 'Mutual friend'. I do my work, take my money, and shut up. Always."

"Not this time."

"How do you know for sure? I'm still breathing, aren't I?"

"You're taking a big chance if you stay here."

"I don't believe you. Get out of here."

Raven lifted the flap of his jacket to show her the .45 under his arm.

"It's not a request, Danielle."

"Holy—" she caught herself, blanching at the sight of the gun. She said, "You're going to kill me if I don't leave? You *claim* to be trying to save me."

"This isn't a debate, Danielle. One way or another, you're getting out of San Francisco *tonight*. It can be comfortable, or not."

He didn't have to bluff any further. Message received. She grabbed a suitcase and makeup case from the closet. He watched her pack in a hurry. It only took a few minutes, most of her time spent in the bathroom gathering up makeup and other necessities. While she packed, he spoke.

"Chelsea Brandt hired you. To trap Kennedy?"

"Yeah. They got a place at the Rincon rigged with cameras. I was supposed to make sure he was filmed."

"Is that what you're usually hired for?"

"I've tricked several guys in the city government, yeah."

"Remember their names?"

"If I see them I will," she said.

She zipped closed her makeup case and flung open a suitcase, which she filled with clothes without bothering to fold anything.

"Are you taking me to the airport?" she said as she zipped the suitcase closed. "Can I get a flight out tonight?"

"Yes, and most likely."

"Guess I can sleep there if not. Who's going to try and kill me in an airport?"

Raven didn't want to mention it remained a distinct possibility regardless.

She grabbed a light jacket and picked up her bags. "Let's go."

In the trip down in the elevator, they rode alone.

"What's going on that makes this different?" she said.

"Have you heard about the dead district attorney?"

"Yeah, so?"

"There's your answer. He was murdered."

"Um...nobody *told* me...no way!"

"Yes way."

"Are you a cop?"

"I'm working with the cops, yes."

It was close to the truth. He looked her in the eye when he said it. She seemed calmer.

The elevator continued down, nearing the lobby.

"What did you do with the video of you and Kennedy?" he said.

"There were two digital files. I put them on a stick drive and gave it to Chelsea. That's *all* I did."

The door rumbled open.

She carried her makeup case and suitcase while Raven kept his hands free. It might not have been chivalrous, but he needed his hands free in case they met trouble. He didn't want trouble. Not in a place so full of people. Not if he could help it.

They waited five minutes for the valet to bring up the Charger. Raven helped get her luggage into the back seat. She climbed into the passenger side while he went around to the wheel.

"SFO?" he said.

"Yeah. There's a 101 Freeway entrance a few blocks up. Go south."

"I know how to get there."

He pulled out of the garage and merged into traffic.

"This is crazy," she said.

"After tomorrow, you won't have anything to worry about."

"Are you sure?"

"Keep an eye on the news, you'll be sure."

She said softly, "Um...okay."

"In the next few days, you'll be contacted by an Inspector named Kayla Blaine. She'll want to know what you told me."

"I'll be waiting."

They drove through an intersection. The freeway entrance lay a block ahead, green signs noting the way.

When another car caught up alongside, Raven shouted, "Get your head down!"

The shotgun blast tore through the rear passenger door, shattering the window. Shards of glass flew into the car, Raven covering his neck, Danielle's scream filling the cabin. She tried to make herself small, the seatbelt preventing her from squeezing into the footwell.

Raven slammed the brakes, the other car speeding by. Raven took off. The enemy car sped up, cutting across lanes, turning sharply down a "buses only" lane and out of sight.

Raven steered for the onramp, speeding up, and gained the freeway.

"It's all right," he said.

"Oh my God they tried to kill me!" She rose from the floor, back onto the seat, yelping, brushing a hand under her. Shards of glass flew off the seat to the floor.

"Buckle up," he said.

She snapped her seatbelt on, almost in a catatonic state. "I don't—"

"Believe it?"

"Oh my God!"

"I wasn't lying to you," Raven said. Cold wind blew into the car, stray pieces of glass still flying from the shattered window.

"Tell your cop friends I will tell them *everything*! I'll *make* shit up if I have to!"

He had to get her to the airport fast and return to the safe house in Marin. He'd left Kayla alone too long already.

But he knew who had the video of Stephen Kennedy.

All the pieces were falling into place.

One more visit. One last arrangement for Kayla's explanation of events, and Raven would finish his mission in San Francisco. The lives of Dixon King and Abelard Joulbert were now in their final moments.

CHAPTER THIRTY-ONE

The man in the van with the submachine gun had a bandage wrapped around the top of his head.

Wexler forced her onto her side, patting down the length of her body, grabbing the SIG Sauer from under her jacket. He didn't stop there. He threw her onto her other side and searched some more. His hands moved fast, not lingering to grope as she'd expect. He was being thorough and professional. Something worse might happen later.

He pulled up the cuffs of her jeans looking for an ankle weapon. She had none. When he let go of her, he sat against the opposite side of the van.

Kayla sat up and scooted away as far as she could. Wexler had the SIG Sauer in the trouser band of his pants.

She looked at the other man. "Cordova?" Kayla said. The man who had punched her in the Tenderloin the night she and Raven had gone looking for the homeless man named Hank.

He smiled at her.

Wexler said, "Figured you two deserved a reunion."

She ignored Wexler and stared at Cordova. "How's the concussion?"

"It'll be better," Cordova said, "when you're dead."

Wexler added, "And your friend. Where is he?"

"You think I'm telling you? Kill me, and you'll never find him. He'll find you."

"He hasn't done much so far except bumble around."

"That's what you think."

"I'm not interested in having a shouting match with you, Inspector. Tell me, or—" He made a fist.

"Bigger men than you have hit me before."

He leaned forward and punched her. The blow took the wind out of her, and all sense, tossing her to her right, toward the passenger seat. The rear of the van had been cleared of seats, leaving only the carpet. The carpet scratched against her hands and face.

"I can keep it up all night," Wexler said.

Still stretched out, Kayla lifted her head high enough to spit blood. "Not what I heard," she snapped. She tasted more on her bottom lip, and her jaw throbbed from the impact.

The van was at freeway speed, starting up an incline. Had to be Highway 101, she realized. From her vantage point, the only road marks visible through the windshield were the bright freeway lampposts. The van was heading out of Marin, into the no man's land between Marin and San Rafael. Nothing but forest on either side of the freeway. Forest and plenty of places to pull off and hide a body. She didn't have much time.

Kayla sat up against the passenger seat, a few feet now separating her and Wexler. He'd have to move forward to get to her again. He'd have to get on his knees. The roof of the van was too low for somebody of his height, even if he managed to talk normally.

She drew her legs up halfway.

As if cocking a pistol.

"You're going to have to kill me, Wexler."

The big man laughed. Cordova laughed. Cordova held

his submachine gun casually, finger off the trigger. Light from roadside lampposts flashed into the interior, letting her capture details. And since Francesco "Frank" Cordova held his submachine gun in his left hand with the muzzle pointing to his right, one such blast of light revealed the safety catch in the ON position.

She had a confined space to fight in, and she needed to make the blows count.

The question was whether she could incapacitate two men twice her size and weight. Wexler had her pistol. He was the obvious first choice to attack.

"I'm not asking nicely again," Wexler said. "You're right, Raven will find us. And we'll be ready for him when he shows up. You two will both be dead within 24 hours and nothing you've done will have mattered."

"Try it."

Wexler's anger flared up, his lips tight, his upper lip twitching as he started forward to grab one of her ankles.

She prayed years of leg presses and marathon running would pay off. She fired her legs like pistons.

She felt a jolt through her body as she connected both feet with Wexler's face. With a startled cry, he fell aside, breaking his fall with both hands on the van floor. His body blocked Cordova's view of her.

She sprang forward as fast as she could, slamming a fist into Wexler's exposed left temple. Another sharp jolt, this one painful, traveled up her right arm, and the blow only stopped him for a moment. He let out an extended groan. She shoved, knocking him off his knees to his side. The SIG Sauer P229 fell from his belt, and she grabbed it with both hands.

Cordova had a clear shot now, yelling to the driver he was going to fire, but Kayla fired first. One shot cracked from the SIG. In the confines of the van, it might as well have been a cannon blast. The .40 caliber slug struck Cordova in the nose, caving in part of his face, and traveling out the back of his head. His body flopped and lay still.

Wexler snapped his eyes to her, reaching out to grab the gun. He batted it away, closing the distance between them, his fiery eyes highlighted by a passing flash of light. She reared back as far as space allowed, pulled the gun close to her body, and worked the trigger again and again. The slugs ripped into Wexler and turned his face into bloody hamburger. He collapsed.

The driver, frantically checking the right mirror as he headed for the side of the road, grabbed for his own gun, but he couldn't shoot and drive at the same time. Kayla slapped a spare magazine into the SIG and shot the driver in the head. Parts of his skull smacked the glass. He dropped his gun and slumped over the wheel. The van continued to veer toward the side of the road.

All she could do now was grab something and hold on. She dropped her gun and grabbed onto the metal frame beneath the passenger seat. It was a lousy grip. The van bumped off the shoulder of the road and started to tip over. The van struck a tree, the violent impact throwing Kayla against one of the bodies. She thought she might die in the van after all.

CHAPTER THIRTY-TWO

Raven shut the door.

"Kayla?"

Silence.

The lights remained on in the living room. She wasn't in the kitchen. Raven hurried through the rest of the house. She wasn't in the bathroom or her bedroom and the M4 Commando he'd placed in the corner of his bedroom hadn't been touched.

He examined the front door. No sign of forced entry. He'd have noted such damage when he used the key. The windows of the house were intact. Kayla was gone, but apparently not because somebody had forcefully entered the house.

Had she answered a knock? No. She would have waited for any visitor to leave. Any visitor with lethal intentions would have forced his way in and to hell with the damage.

He sat on the couch with his shoulders slumped, his mind numb. What had happened? Leaving her had been a mistake. Why hadn't he insisted on her coming with him?

Getting Danielle Rawlings to San Francisco International Airport had been easy, and he'd left her at the departure terminal to return to Las Vegas. He wasn't sure what to do with the shotgun-damaged Charger yet, but now he had another crisis. Where was Kayla?

He searched the house again, this time for her purse and key to the place and found neither. Had she left on her own? A walk to clear her head? Should he drive around the neighborhood looking for her?

Had she decided to go to San Francisco? Maybe to confront Captain Marty Dresnik?

His mind raced. He needed time to think. Hopping in the shower, he spent five minutes washing the night away, and dried off and put on new clothes. He strapped his shoulder rig with the Nighthawk .45 across his back.

Kayla had not returned during his shower.

He sat at the kitchen table with a cup of tea, watching the steam.

He was now facing the worst-case scenario.

She was gone and he was on his own.

Evidence didn't matter anymore. Only vengeance. He could strike at the heart of Dixon King's empire and bring the man to his knees and put a bullet through his head.

The last person he wanted to talk to, the King lieutenant by the name of Tyrone Biggins, was still valid. He didn't know where to find King, and rattling cages to uncover the gangster might not go as planned if he took a bullet along the way. But Biggins, who had spilled information to Charlie Kline at the start of the mess, would know where King lived. He'd tell Raven where to go.

He'd go to Biggins' night club, Teaser. He'd know who to look for because Oscar Morey had sent a picture from the man's rap sheet. They would talk, and if Biggins didn't give up the information, Raven had no problem using a bit of pressure.

He had nothing to lose now.

Nothing to do but take action.

But he felt drained as he sat there. His body did not respond to his command to move. He could try and sleep, but doubted he'd be able to rest.

Maybe if he gave Kayla more time...

A key rattled in the lock.

He eyes flashed to the door, but he didn't go for the .45. The key scratched again, and he heard it drop, followed by a cry of frustration. A feminine cry. A woman! *Kayla!*

He ran to the door and pulled it open.

Kayla Blaine, on her hands and knees on the porch, looked up at him with pleading eyes.

Her hair was a mess. Her lower lip bulged red. Her older bruise seemed to throb, and sweat covered her body, her clothes clinging to her skin.

Raven scooped her up in his arms, kicked the door shut, and brought her into her bedroom where he set her gently on the bed. She curled up and sobbed.

He didn't talk. He moved hair away from her face.

She cried for several minutes, and finally wiped her eyes and took a deep breath. Rolling onto her back, she looked at him with glazed eyes.

"Wexler's dead."

Raven flinched. "How?"

She explained her ordeal in detail. Raven asked where her purse was. She said she must have dropped it on the porch. Raven ran for it, found the purse where she said, and closed and locked the door. He tossed the purse on the kitchen counter.

In the room, he found her sitting up on the bed.

"You should stay down." He sat beside her and put an arm around her. She leaned her head against his shoulder.

"I'll be okay. Few bumps and bruises. I'm fine."

"Your lip looks bad."

"I've had worse."

He laughed. From the lowest low, the woman who had

impressed him earlier broke through the fog.

"I need a shower."

"I'll put coffee on."

She left him, grabbing the thin pink bathrobe out of her tote, and went down the hall.

Raven made coffee in the kitchen and took a moment to sort through the information in the manila envelope. He found photocopies of FBI files, some marked confidential, and frowned. Why would Cindy Chu provide this? Regardless of the answer, Raven found a wealth of information.

Guns stored at various warehouses. He wondered if the crates he'd seen at the warehouse when he first arrived had held small arms and explosives. It was good to know. He made a mental note of the locations.

Information on business fronts, locations for illegal gambling, prostitution, drug distribution. It was all there in black and white courtesy of the United States government.

Kayla finished her shower and wandered into the kitchen in the pink bathrobe. It fit her figure well. Her wet hair stayed behind her head. She accepted the coffee he offered, gingerly trying to sip, but her lip didn't cause much discomfort, so she drank. She sat on a stool next to him.

Raven gestured to the spread of papers across the counter. "Why did your friend give you this?"

"She says they know you."

"How do they know me?"

"Well enough they want you to have this stuff. We didn't talk much about it, Sam. Maybe the FBI realizes a different 'instrument of justice' is required here."

"We have it all, except where Dixon King lives."

She took another sip of the coffee. "Should be in there."

Raven searched through the papers once more, catching a few he'd missed on his first pass. Eventually he found what he wanted. An address in Marin, but unfortunately no pictures. He found pictures by looking up the address on his phone and examining a satellite view of the house.

The rear side faced a cliff overlooking the ocean and the Golden Gate Bridge. A wall kept the property separate from the cliff drop-off, but not a high wall. Well-maintained yard from wall to patio.

Raven's strategic mind was already firing. The lack of energy prior to Kayla's return had vanished. Now he was ready to fight again and bring the battle to a proper conclusion.

"What are you thinking?" she said.

"Ever hear of Tyrone Biggins?"

She shook her head.

"Charlie Kline talked about him as a primary source, the reason he started trying to blow the whistle on the alliance and the murder of Whitlow. Biggins is one of King's people."

"Why would he talk to a reporter?"

"That's what I want to know. For some reason, Biggins is willing to spill his guts. What we need to do is ask if he'll become a federal witness, and help you explain your way out of this mess when it's over."

"Because you're not going to be here."

"It's in my best interest I'm not here, Kayla."

She put her coffee mug down.

"You're sure he knows what you think he knows?" she said.

"He didn't know about Chelsea Brandt," Raven admitted, "at least not at the time or Charlie would have said so. But he knew enough to get Charlie started."

"Wait." She held up a hand. "What's this about Chelsea Brandt? Is she King's candidate?"

Raven laughed. "We've been so focused on your ordeal I had no chance to tell you about my night."

He filled her in from beginning to end.

Kayla shook her head when he finished. "Wow. This runs deeper than I thought. Will Danielle be of any help?"

"She's waiting for your call. She promised to tell you what she told me, and even make up something if she had to."

Kayla smiled. "How nice of her."

"But seriously, yes. She'll testify. She always suspected it was the mafia she did those jobs for, including Kennedy, but never saw any faces. She can for sure say Chelsea Brandt is the one who made the deal with her. It's all you need."

Kayla nodded. "Then when we grill Chelsea—"

"It all comes out in the wash."

He looked at her. Cleaned up, she didn't look too bad. The lip would swell a bit more, but it wouldn't kill her. The bruise would certainly fade after a week or two.

She looked small sitting on the stool in her bathrobe with her hair wet.

"One more day," Raven said, "and it's over."

"I think I'm going to be okay," she said.

"You will. Now we should get some rest."

She laughed. "After coffee?"

"You'll be surprised how quickly you'll pass out."

They left the kitchen. He made the mistake of walking to the bedroom with her.

CHAPTER THIRTY-THREE

He said goodnight as she stepped through the doorway, but she turned around to face him.

A switch flipped within both of them, and she threw her arms around him, and he grabbed her in return, pulling her warm fragile body against his, their kiss intense, Kayla letting out a moan as her tender lower lip flared, and they broke the kiss, but didn't stop. He grabbed her with both arms below her bottom, lifting her off the floor and dropping her onto the bed. She bounced on landing, reaching for the strap holding the robe closed, flinging both sides open.

He straddled her and leaned down for another kiss, not a hard one this time, moving along her chin, down to her neck as she tipped her head back. She was breathing hard. "Please, more," she said.

He felt the rush of her heartbeat beneath him as he ran his hands from her hips, feeling the soft curves, across her stomach, cupping her breasts softly, Kayla pulling him tight to her so he couldn't get away.

Her hands moved fast, undoing his belt, his shirt; he had to stop to get his shoes off, but they didn't stop for long. She spread her legs and reached between them to help guide him

228 | BRIAN DRAKE

into her. They were two bodies moving against each other, but together at the same time, and when they reached their peak, time stood still and only the beating of their hearts filled their senses.

She stretched out beside him as he lay on his back, catching his breath, putting her head on his chest as it rose and fell. He brushed her hair away from her face.

"I needed that," she said. "I don't care if it's wrong."

"Not wrong," he said, "only temporary."

"I'll take temporary," she said. "It's all we have right now."

Raven stared at the ceiling as she fell asleep and began to snore lightly.

When it was all over, she'd go back to her life, and he'd go back to his. But as he lay beneath her, he knew she had more to return to than he'd ever have again.

It was the choice he'd made. The one he had to live with.

She looked bright and happy at breakfast, makeup covering the bruise, but there was nothing to do about the fat lip.

She cooked breakfast and they ate at the kitchen table. They said nothing about the previous night. There was no need to do so.

Raven studied the FBI information after finishing the pancakes she made.

"This is interesting," he said.

"What?"

"The FBI says if King doesn't pull off this alliance, he's out. Out, as in dead. The mob commission on New York City won't tolerate failure. This operation stands to bring in billions and they want those billions *badly*."

"They'll need to force out a lot of competition up and down the coast."

"Hence the guns in the warehouses," he said. "Enough for a small army."

He passed her the pages as he finished reading them.

They cleaned and stacked the dishes and she said, "Now we go see Tyrone Biggins?"

"Yes," he said. "With a conspicuous car."

"Don't worry about it," she said. "It won't be the first time anybody around San Francisco has seen bullet holes."

"Shotgun, dear."

"Whatever."

They agreed on a plan. Raven would go through the front door, while Kayla entered through the back.

Club Tease sat on Essex so close to the Bay Bridge that a portion of the 80 Skyway to the span passed over the building. In the late afternoon, the traffic noise was intense, the street below equally packed. Raven and Kayla approached on foot, walking up a slight incline to the closed club. Closed for business, but there was work going on inside to prepare for the evening opening.

An empty lot next to the club, fenced off from the sidewalk, was Kayla's entrance. She slipped through an opening in the fence and cut through the lot to the rear of the Tease building.

Raven walked up to the front door like he owned the place.

Target: Tyrone Biggins.

Objective: Make him talk and agree to testify.

Raven rapped on the door. The sign behind the glass said CLOSED.

A man in an apron approached the glass. "We're closed!"

"I need to see Tyrone."

"He's not here."

Raven played a hunch. "Tell him it's Wexler."

"Who?"

"Wexler!"

The man in the apron nodded and retreated the way he'd come. Apparently, he'd never seen Leonard Wexler in the flesh, but knew the name well enough to move his keister at any mention.

Raven moved to the side so he was only partially visible through the glass. Tyrone Biggins walked toward him, wearing a suit minus the jacket. He looked about Raven's height and half his bulk.

The door opened outward, further concealing Raven until the last second, when he swung around and pushed the .45 into Biggins' belly.

"Hey, what is this?"

"Get inside."

"Got no money here, man."

"I want to talk about Charlie Kline."

They were inside, the door slamming shut.

Raven said, "I'll put the iron away. I want to talk about Kline."

Biggins stared blankly and exhaled in what seemed like relief.

"I thought I was alone," Biggins said. "Who are you?"

Raven holstered the .45. "A friend."

Commotion in the kitchen. Yelling. Kayla identifying herself as a police officer.

"I have another friend," Raven added, "coming in the back."

Biggins turned to look where Raven indicated. Kayla appeared in the doorway of the kitchen, badge hanging around her neck. "SFPD," she said. "You Biggins?"

"Yes, ma'am."

Raven said, "Can we talk in your office?"

"Looks like you got me covered at both ends."

"Looks like," Raven said.

"My office is this way, come on."

The office was small but tidy, and Biggins invited Kayla to sit in the only other available chair while Raven leaned against the doorframe.

"When they got Charlie, I thought I was next," Biggins said. His eyes darted between Raven and Kayla. "He tell you about me?"

Kayla looked at Raven. "Your cue."

Raven explained his meeting with Charlie Kline, adding details about the efforts he and Kayla had made against King and the French, including the death of Wexler the previous night.

Biggins seemed to sink in the chair as he heard the story. He carried a great weight, Raven could tell. He was a man who wanted to get the weight off his chest.

"Charlie was a good man," Biggins said. "I liked him a lot."

"What made you trust him?"

"He was a viper. Kid wanted to change things. I thought he could pull it off if he had help, you know? Somebody on the inside who knew things. Otherwise, he'd have been hit by a truck long before he actually got killed."

"The real question, Tyrone," Raven said, "is why you wanted to talk to him in the first place."

Biggins leaned over to a corner of the desk and turned a framed photograph so Raven and Kayla could see. The picture showed Biggins and a pregnant woman, her face beaming, his hands on her belly.

"That's my wife," Biggins said, choking on the words a little. He cleared his throat. "That was our baby."

"Was?"

"Died in the crib." When Biggins looked at Raven, he was on the verge of years. "Just happened, you know? We put him down for the night and woke up because it was too quiet. He wasn't crying at three a.m. We found him on his side, and he was gone."

Biggins regarded both of them sadly, his eyes on Kayla as he said, "It was like somebody turned off a light. Gone." He snapped his fingers. "Like that."

Raven nodded.

Biggins' shoulders sank some more. He dropped his eyes to his desk. "After we buried my son, I thought long and hard about things. I got to thinking—"

"What?" Raven prompted.

"Maybe God was punishing me for the things I've done. He took my son because of me not being a good person." He looked up, exasperated. "I run this club for the mob, get it? The money goes to Dixon King, the *kingpin* of San Francisco. We sell *drugs* here. We launder money. We got hookers. We do it all, man. It finally caught up with me."

Biggins fiddled with a pen on the desktop, set it aside. "Can't go to the cops because they're dirty. I thought if I could get a story in the press, somebody might pay attention. I could tell the FBI. Know what my problem was?"

"Tell me," Raven said.

"They're always watching. You can't take a piss without the boss knowing about it, and he's way the hell away from here." He started counting off on fingers. "I was scared, I was angry, I was hurting, and I didn't know what else to do. That's when I found Charlie Kline at a donut shop, of all places."

"How did you recognize him?"

"He was interviewing the owner about his life story. Guy came all the way over from some back-ass dirt-poor country and made good selling donuts in San Francisco. Can you believe it?"

Kayla took over. "Tyrone, are you willing to testify to what you know about the criminal activity of Dixon King?"

"You promise to keep me alive if I do?"

"It won't be the SFPD taking your statement. We'll be going to the FBI."

"We? You and me?"

"That's right."

Biggins pointed at Raven. "What about hunky dude right there?"

Kayla laughed. "Hunky dude," she said, "is going to make sure you can tell us your story without fear of reprisal."

Biggins turned to Raven. "How you gonna do that?"

"Dixon King's life will be over before the sun comes up tomorrow, Tyrone. You have my word. When he goes, the rest of his crew will shoot each other trying to take over the chair, and in the chaos, the FBI swoops in, based on what you tell them, and what others witnesses we have tell them, and we can clean up this city for good."

Biggins laughed. "You'll clean it up for ten minutes. It will get dirty all over again. People in charge here? They don't know how to live without being on the take."

"What do you know about the French alliance?"

"Heard a little."

Raven nodded. "The DA's race?"

"We got that blonde babe Brandt sewn up tight. She'll do whatever she's told."

"Excellent." Raven said to Kayla. "Your case is sitting right there, Inspector. You have the girl in Nevada, too, and you can flip Chelsea Brandt easily. Think it's enough?"

Kayla said to Tyrone, "One more thing. Your contact at the Southern Station. Martin Dresnik?"

"Yeah."

Kayla looked like she wanted to cry. "That's plenty," she told Raven.

Raven and Kayla looked at each other sadly. This would be the last time they saw each other. They acknowledged the truth quietly between them. She had work to do.

And so did he.

CHAPTER THIRTY-FOUR

At 6:45 in the evening, a fire broke out at a warehouse on the Central Waterfront in San Francisco's Dogpatch neighborhood. The fire department responded with four engine crews, but the blaze consumed the warehouse and the contents within.

When firemen put out the fire, they found two men dead. Both shot, each with submachine guns strapped to their upper bodies.

Police found the remains of over a dozen crates inside, all containing military-grade small arms. Rifles, pistols, explosives. Some of the crates were open. Cops speculated they had been opened before the fire.

As the clock struck eight o'clock, Sam Raven steered the rented Charger up a winding hill in Marin. Grassy hills and trees flashed by on either side of the two-lane road. He parked on the shoulder before the top of the hill and went the rest of the way on foot. He moved fast, dressed in black, his face streaked with black combat cosmetics. A black wool cap sat on his head; the Nighthawk .45 secured under his right arm. A chest rig over the shoulder harness containing more deadly tools of the trade.

Across his chest, 30-round magazines for the Colt M4 Commando, suppressor attached. The carbine was slung across his back.

New additions to the rig, courtesy of the Dogpatch weapons stash of Dixon King, hung on the rig via clips: six fragmentation grenades, and two smoke grenades.

A sheathed combat knife rode on his right hip.

He was ready for war, and he was going to bring war to Dixon King.

He ran up the hill, legs pumping, lungs straining, sweating with the effort. Once he reached the trees providing cover from the roadway, he allowed himself to stop and rest.

The plan: approach the King house from the cliff side, hop over the wall, and begin his assault.

Fire and fury.

And no mercy.

Raven waited for darkness to take its stranglehold on the night, staying flat in the trees, listening. The wind was a constant companion and carried sound along with the breeze. Traffic from the bridge drifted to him. Critters moved about. Crickets began their evening broadcasts. Nature had settled.

Raven rose from his position, unslung the M4 Commando, and moved out.

He could slip off the rocks any second, and the fall into the ocean would end his crusade forever.

He moved carefully along the narrow pathway. The jagged hillside, full of sharp boulders planted deep in the earth, threatened at each step. Waves crashed below. Still his stomach lurched at the drop. If the enemy caught him on his way in, he wouldn't survive either.

The King mansion lay ahead, another fifteen yards, one side

of the protective wall in sight.

Raven's slow movement made the ten yards seem like ten miles. Eventually he reached the wall, the top part of the house now in view, and risked a peek over the top.

The immaculate lawn spread out behind the house, hemmed in by the wall stretching around the property. The lawn ended at a patio, the border between the two marked by trees and a pair of hedgerows with a gap of about six feet between them. The lawn wrapped around both sides of the house to the front.

The patio. Pool and hot tub, the pool centered perfectly, the hot tub under the overhanging patio extending from the master bedroom. Sliding glass doors led from the patio into the house. A lower-level garage with guest suite on top extended from the house on Raven's right.

Two gunners rounded the far corner beneath the master bedroom. They were met by a third who crossed from the guest house, having completed a circuit at the front. The three exchanged a few words. They carried submachine guns of the Heckler & Koch UMP variety.

How many more inside? How many at the front? They wouldn't expect Raven to attack from the rear.

If they had a rotating cadre, perhaps three more at the front, and six more inside on standby for their patrols. And the guns suggested they were waiting for trouble.

In fact, expecting trouble.

Wayne, the house guard, once again left his office inside the house to check on the troops.

Dixon King was upstairs in his bedroom office talking with the three Frenchman. He didn't want to be there. Nobody had looked happy before the meeting began.

Wayne wished they had more men to cover things, and more hardware, but he had to work with what he had.

What he did have were two guys in front, one at the top of the front steps, another at the three-car-garage around the side of the house.

Two more worked the main gate at the bottom of the driveway, out of sight.

Three worked the rear. King didn't expect an attack from the rear. He thought the cliff protected that side of the house. Wayne, an Iraqi war vet, figured the enemy would count on that, so he put an extra shooter back there. Seven shooters outside, three more inside, and him. Against one man. They didn't need an army to fight this Sam Raven bastard, but Wayne had a nagging sense that he didn't have enough guys.

He checked on the shooter at the porch, walked down the drive to the gate, then back up to the rear. When he found the three shooters in back chatting, he yelled for them to quit wasting time and get back on watch.

The problem was his shooters hadn't seen real combat. Ever. Shooting at stationary targets wasn't training, despite the courses of fire Wayne set up forcing them to use cover and concealment while.

Wayne adjusted the sling holding his HK low at his hip. He'd seen enough action to know he could handle himself, but he needed his men to step up too.

He scanned the wall at the end of the lawn, saw no sign of trouble there.

Maybe the boss was right. Any attack would come from the front. Trying to move along the side of the mountain, no matter how careful a trained operator took the steps, was suicide.

Raven smiled as he squatted. He'd lowered his head before the boss saw him. He was too busy yelling at his guys to look. Now he knew who was in charge, a thin fellow with blond hair, white shirt and trousers, HK UMP like the rest of the gunners.

He removed one of the smoke grenades from his chest rig and pulled the pin.

Time for war.

It was the worst of all possible meetings.

What to do now. What they had worked for was falling to pieces.

Dixon King, in his suit, paced his den on the first floor of the house. Abelard Joulbert sat on a couch with his two lieutenants close by. They wore guns under their suit jackets. King hadn't bothered to remember their names.

News of Leonard Wexler's death had filtered in earlier in the morning. Dresnik confirmed the story through sources with the Marin County Sheriff's Department. The bodies recovered from the wrecked van were indeed Leonard Wexler and Francesco Cordova. The woman was not with them, which meant she was with Raven. The net was circling around King and the clock was running out.

It had been going so well. Whitlow's death. The silencing of Kline and the hooker who started the mess. The election was the next day. The Kennedy video would have gone out in time for the six o'clock news, but there was no reason now.

Everything they'd worked for would have come to fruition. But Kayla Blaine and Sam Raven remained the only two forces able to stop him, and now they had the help of the FBI.

All this he had explained to Joulbert, who now responded after a period of quiet thought.

"What do they have as proof? Evidence?"

"We tried to cut Raven and Blaine off at every opportunity, but maybe they found something. All they'd need is a thread to pull on, enough to explain away the bodies, because you said so yourself, Abelard. Sam Raven doesn't need proof."

"Seems to me," Joulbert said, "the only thing for us to do is cut our losses."

"That means you going back to France to face certain death, and me, too."

"We can run."

"We can't run far enough."

"Final option, in that case."

"What?"

"Wait for Raven to come and kill us. And hope we can kill him first."

"I got a bunch of guys standing around here waiting for that to happen. Maybe it will. Maybe we'll get lucky."

But Dixon King had never believed in anything as flimsy as hope. Reaching behind his back, he took out his Smith & Wesson Model 60. The snub-nosed stainless-steel revolver didn't seem like much, but it's all he had between him and doomsday. He checked the load and put the gun away.

Let the bastard come and get me!

Raven let the pin on the smoke grenade pop and stood for an overhand pitch.

The canister hissed out thick white smoke halfway through its arc, landing on the grass, rolling. The smoke created a thick cloud that spread throughout the yard.

Raven leaped over the wall.

Men were already shouting, sounding the alarm, firing sporadic shots into the smoke. None hit Raven as he charged into the smoke, grabbing one of his high explosive frag grenades.

He cleared the smoke, emerging like a wraith, and flung the grenade at two of the gunmen beneath the upper patio. His eyes tracked the third, bringing up the M4 Commando as he continued running for the hedge.

The grenade exploded in a bright orange flash, wiping out the two shooters, leaving black scaring on the walls. Raven settled the red dot of his optic on the third shooter, who brought his weapon up, but not fast enough. A suppressed trio of rounds from Raven's carbine tore his chest open, sending him falling forward in a heap.

The thick smoke continued to drift, but slowly, gaps in the haze opening. Raven pivoted right. Men shouting from the guest house. Two gunners, one at the corner, the other breaking for a tree. Raven tracked the runner, firing, missed. He dropped before the shooter at the corner opened fire, the chattering of his HK crackling through the night. Raven snapped a shot and tore chunks of plaster out of the wall beside the shooter's head. The man screamed, falling back, exposing himself to Raven's follow-up shot that took him down.

Raven bolted forward, cutting through the gap in the hedges, landing hard on the concrete. The second shooter fired around the tree truck, one side, the other, unable to spot his target through the drifting smoke. Raven pitched another grenade. The blast took down the tree and the man behind it, the upper trunk of the tree falling on top of the man's body.

Raven rose, checking for more shooters, he spun to cover his left side. Two more moving in, following the outer wall, using bushes on that side for concealment.

Raven stayed near the hedges, watching the gunners' movements over the top. The hedges wouldn't stop a bullet, and the smoke began to thin as it dissipated with the coastal breeze. Raven had to work fast. He rose high enough to shoot, firing two single shots. Somebody yelled but didn't fall, but one of the gunners left the wall for another tree. Raven snapped off a shot. The gunner's head jerked, his body dropping in a pile.

Raven jumped over the hedge as the other shooter returned fire, the shots tearing into the hedge, Raven landing on the grass with the M4 Commando tight to his shoulder and the red dot sight fixed on his target. The M4's stock kicked against his shoulder twice. Man down, crushing the bushes beneath his body.

Raven's boots scraped the patio as he threaded between the pool and hot tub. Another burst from the M4 took out the sliding glass doors. He ducked as he ran through, bits of glass falling onto his back before dropping onto the carpet.

Family room. Expensive furniture. Raven dropped behind a couch to slap another 30-round mag into the M4 Commando's magwell. He stayed put, listening.

Somebody was yelling. From where, Raven had no idea. But the voice was loud. Close. Maybe the front of the house.

It was happening!

That Raven bastard had come over the wall. The hell with the cliff. The turkey had guts; Wayne had to admit that.

He summoned the last three shooters, telling them the stairway was their battle line. Nobody could get past them and up the stairs. The nervous shooters agreed. Wayne bolted up the curving steps to the hallway above, where he ran to King's bedroom. He the boss and the Frenchmen huddled behind furniture.

"What's going on?" King said from behind a couch.

"He's here!"

"I *get* that, what's our status?"

"He's in the house!"

Two of the Frenchmen, the assistants to Abelard Joulbert, had pistols in their hands. Wayne was glad for a few extra guns.

He wondered if they would be enough.

"Watch the door!" King shouted.

Wayne nodded and dropped low in the doorway, his eyes on the other end of the hall. If the guys in the foyer failed, he was the last line of defense. Only his gun stood between Sam Raven and eternity, not only for him, but his boss and the French as well.

No more shouting. But Raven heard the orders and knew at least one shooter was waiting by the stairway.

He moved around the couch, scanning for danger. The large family room led to a hall. Raven stayed at the corner, peeked around, drew his head back. Clear. He rounded the corner, muzzle ahead. Doorway on his right. He slipped into the room, checked left, swung right. Dining area. Empty. He stepped out into the hall again.

Whoever had designed the house went big on white. The walls and tiles matched, but the tiles were shiny marble. Archway ahead. Raven caught partial sight of the front door. That's where the stairway would be. And at least one shooter waiting in ambush.

Feet shuffled. Whispers. Raven paused. More than one. He crossed to the left wall, staying close, inching forward two feet at a time. Paused, listened. No more whispers. Two more feet. Closer to the corner. His pulse pounded in his head. He stopped midway and selected another grenade. Pulling the pin, he pitched it hard. The grenade bounced off the wall beside the doorway, flying back at an angle and out of sight.

The blast shook the house. Raven hustled to the corner, stopped, flashed around with his carbine probing for targets.

One man lay in the center of the foyer, his body split open, skin blacked. Smoke hung in the room. Raven skidded backward to the safety of the corner once again. Who had the man been talking to?

Rounding the corner one step at a time, Raven probed with the muzzle of the Colt carbine. Still no sign of another shooter. An area beneath the staircase was shrouded in shadow. Raven fired twice into the opening and scored a hit, two wet slaps. A gunner tumbled into view and fell flat on his face.

Raven started for the staircase, swinging the carbine up to follow the bannister. He checked his stride as a third shooter opened fire, his HK spitting flame.

Raven rolled forward as the stingers wreaked havoc around him, chewing into the marble. Raven jumped up, slipping on blood. He fell hard, rolling under the staircase as another salvo crashed. Raven couldn't see the shooter, but he swung his carbine and fired twice, then broke for another doorway a few feet away. He dived through the doorway.

He rolled out of view, rising again to press his back to the wall.

Another hallway, open at either end, the hall he'd come through on one side, another room on the other. Antique swords hung on the walls.

The third shooter yelled for help as he descended the steps. Raven swung through the doorway, catching the gunner as his feet touched the marble tiles. He fired twice. The gunman let out another yell as the .223 sizzlers ripped him open. He spun like a top, landing with his legs and arms twisted under him.

Raven reloaded. The mag wasn't empty, but he wanted a full charge when he reached the top floor. He moved for the staircase, stepping around the corpse on the floor, and started climbing.

Reaching the second-floor hall, he knelt and listened. Voices. English. French. King and Joulbert. He peeked around the corner and pulled his head back. A burst of submachine gun fire smacked into the wall, tearing out chunks of plaster. A gunner squatted in a doorway at the far end.

The shooting stopped. Raven let the silence grow a moment. Then: "Dixon King!"

"Is that you, Raven!"

"Come out and die like a man!"

"Never!"

King barked an order, there was a short argument, and another SMG burst ripped Raven's way.

Raven rolled into the hall, staying flat as he came up on his belly. The gunman in the doorway, the blond in the white shirt, tracked him. The red dot on the Aimpoint optic settled on the gunner's head as he dropped his empty HK and pulled a pistol. The M4 chugged one round. The gunner's head popped. He fell, his body blocking the doorway.

More yelling, in French this time.

Raven jumped up and ran the rest of the way, leaping over the body, turning into the master bedroom. He swept right-to-left, his trigger finger pumping. The M4 Commando spat in quick succession. Two French gunners fell with their guns in their hands, Abelard Joulbert making a desperate grab for a fallen pistol as Raven stitched a burst through his neck, almost cutting off his head. As he completed the sweep, Dixon King dived behind a couch. Raven shot the couch, the cushions splitting open, spraying stuffing.

King shouted, "Stop!"

"Get up!"

Dixon King rose with his hands in the air. He came around the couch.

"I don't have a gun, Raven. You going to murder an unarmed man?"

Raven grinned. "Bet your ass."

Raven let the M4 drop on its sling, reaching for the combat knife on his right hip as Dixon King made his move.

He reached behind his under his suit jacket and drew a

stainless-steel revolver. Raven admired the effort as he closed the distance, batting the pistol away. He plunged the knife deep into King's belly.

Dixon King howled; his face twisted with pain. He slapped both hands to Raven's wrist, trying to pull the knife out. Blood seeped between his fingers as the fluid rushed from his body. Raven pulled out the knife and dropped it, grabbing King under both arms. He dragged King through the next room where doors opened onto the upper patio.

Dixon King continued to wail, struggling to break Raven's grip and keep his insides from coming out at the same time. He didn't have the strength for both.

Raven slid the balcony door open and dragged King outside.

He reached the wall, grunting with effort. Grabbing King between the legs, Raven hauled him over the top of the wall and let gravity take over.

King fell fast.

A big splash of water. Raven rested both hands on the top of the wall and leaned over. King had gone face first into his hot tub, striking his head on the bottom. His body was still, feet sticking out, resting against the edge of the tub, the water filling with a red cloud.

Raven exhaled a sigh of satisfaction.

It wasn't supposed to end like this!

The thought passed through King's mind as he plummeted to the ground.

I was supposed to die in bed a rich man. King of the kingpins. Top of the heap.

The last thing he saw was the water in the hot tub, growing larger as he neared. He closed his eyes.

Dixon King never felt the impact.

CHAPTER THIRTY-FIVE

Headquarters was the safest place.

The warehouse fire in the Dogpatch neighborhood meant one thing to Dresnik. The end approaching.

Unable to reach King, he left his house and drove to Southern Station headquarters, where he sat in his office. The late-night crew had cleared out of the squad room to hit the street. Plenty of work tonight, plenty of homicides to attend to. Good cops doing what they did best. Dresnik loved his crew. He loved being a cop. But somewhere along the way, he'd compromised one too many times.

He'd give anything to take back those compromises, but it was too late for second chances.

He sat alone at his cluttered desk. There was still so much to do, the work never ending. He sweated, drinking water to compensate, trying to calm his nerves.

The squad room door opened.

He looked up.

And now the end.

Inspector Kayla Blaine entered first, followed by Special Agent Cindy Chu of the Federal Bureau of Investigation. Two other special agents, men, followed. Their eyes landed on him as if he were a great white buffalo and they were hunters on safari.

Kayla took the lead. She stopped in his office doorway, as she had so many times before.

She said, "I'm going to give you one opportunity to tell me it isn't true, Marty."

"What happened to you, Kayla?"

"I have your friends to thank for this lip, Captain. But it will heal."

Dresnik stared at her. The FBI agents stared at him. Kayla was the only one who showed emotion. She looked hurt, betrayed, looking for any reason not to believe the things she'd learned, or come to suspect.

"Are you going to tell me it's not true, Captain?"

"It's all true."

Kayla took a deep breath, let it out, and stepped aside.

Agent Chu and her men stepped forward.

"Martin Dresnik, you're under arrest for conspiracy to commit murder, and a variety of other charges but we'll be here all night if you want me to list them. Stand up."

Dresnik stood. The two male agents rushed him, grabbing his service revolver and badge, wrenching his arms behind him. He felt the metal of the handcuffs biting hard into his wrists. He grunted at the sharp pain. So this is what it felt like. How many perps had he put the cuffs on in his years as a cop?

They pushed him around his desk, through the doorway. He passed Kayla, turning his head to see her.

"I'm sorry, Kayla."

The agents took him out of the squad room.

Inspector Kayla Blaine stood alone in the squad room with Cindy Chu. Cindy gave her a half-smile.

"It's over," she said.

"Yeah."

"You okay?"

"I feel numb. I can't think right now."

"Let's get him booked, and I'll take you home. Okay?"

Home.

The word sounded nice.

Raven found King's wall safe in the ground floor office. It took a few minutes listening for the tumblers to fall as he turned the knob, but he finally turned the handle and wrenched the safe open.

Among the folders inside, and the cash and automatic pistol, he found an envelope with KENNEDY scrawled across the front. He looked inside and found the USB memory stick. He put it in a pocket and grabbed the stacks of cash and stuffed his other pockets full. There wasn't anything else of interest.

He found a board on the wall of the kitchen with car keys. Grabbing one, he unlocked a gray Mercedes in the garage. There were two other cars there, a Lamborghini and McLaren. He ignored them as he fired up the Mercedes and pressed the button on the remote connected to the visor. The garage door opened.

As he drove away, passing the Charger where he'd left it, he smiled. His exit was far more comfortable than his entrance.

Cindy Chu dropped Kayla off at her apartment building and told her to get some rest. She needed to be at the FBI office at nine a.m. sharp. They had a lot to sort through, and it would take several days.

Kayla rode up the elevator to her floor. She'd left her things behind at the AirBNB in Marin, but she still had the key. She could go back for them. Returning to the house, and remembering Raven there with her, might be difficult, but she was a big girl. She could handle it. After the last few days, she knew she could handle anything.

At her door, she fitted the key into the lock and turned the knob, stepping inside.

She froze. The lights were on. She felt somebody's presence. Dropping the keys in her pocket, she took out her gun and moved forward.

Sam Raven sat on the couch. He looked silly in black, his face still painted, but his smile lit up his face.

"I found the video of Stephen Kennedy," he said. "It's on the kitchen table there."

Speechless, she put her gun away.

"I'm sure you can figure out something to do with it. Maybe tell the poor jerk he doesn't have to worry about it anymore. Or don't," he added. "It might be nice to have dirt on the new district attorney."

He rose and approached her. She smiled, tears filling her eyes. They blurred her vision, so she wiped her eyes, and Raven was still there, closer now.

"Hey," he said. "You didn't think I'd leave without a proper goodbye, did you?"

She let him wrap her in his arms and squeezed him tight in return.

"I could use a place to stay tonight," he said into her ear.

"My bed's big enough for two," she said.

Raven's jet left SFO the next morning.

Raven sat alone in first class. He stared out the window as the ground fell away and the plane climbed into the clouds. He'd left Kayla Blaine behind at the airport. Their last goodbye had been brief. And tough on them both.

But it was time to put San Francisco behind him. He left many bodies there, and a piece of his heart too.

He hoped other lives he didn't know about may have been saved along with Kayla's, but he regretted not being able to do more. His thoughts lingered on Charlie Kline and Margot Hensley; Hank, the homeless witness; Sergeant Lori Morgan; the other cops he hadn't learned the names of. Victims in an everlasting war showing no signs of ceasing.

He'd carry the pain with him, as he always did, and learn to live with the ghosts. He couldn't save everybody, but he'd never stop trying to save the ones he could as he followed the wind around the world.

He wondered where the wind might take him next as he asked for a Maker's Mark on the rocks from the flight attendant. As the liquor warmed his stomach, all he knew for sure was the next time was coming soon, because monsters lurked in the shadow, and he needed to find them. But now, for a moment, he could rest.

WATCH FOR LADY DEATH
(A SAM RAVEN THRILLER)

THOUSANDS OF LIVES ARE AT STAKE, AND SAM RAVEN MAY HAVE MET HIS MATCH!

Tanya Jafari, an operative for the Islamic Union, comes to Sam Raven seeking help. In exchange for protection from the CIA, she'll tell all she knows about the growing terrorist group.

Raven's skepticism ends when an assassin tries to kill her. Before it's too late, he brings Tanya to the US for debriefing. The CIA wants to kill the leader of the Islamic Union, a woman called the White Widow, and Tanya knows where she's hiding.

But Tanya holds another secret close to her chest, knowledge of a threat so large it will shake world governments and bring the West to its knees. And it may be too late to stop. . .

From the author of the Scott Stiletto series comes a new hero. Sam Raven is grittier, deadlier, and you better not stand in his way.

AVAILABLE MAY 2021

ABOUT THE AUTHOR

A twenty-five year veteran of radio and television broad-casting, Brian Drake has spent his career in San Francisco where he's filled writing, producing, and reporting duties with stations such as KPIX-TV, KCBS, KQED, among many others. Currently carrying out sports and traffic reporting duties for Bloomberg 960, Brian Drake spends time between reports and carefully guarded morning and evening hours cranking out action/adventure tales. A love of reading when he was younger inspired him to create his own stories, and he sold his first short story, "The Desperate Minutes," to an obscure webzine when he was 25 (more years ago than he cares to remember, so don't ask).

Drake lives in California with his wife and two cats, and when he's not writing he is usually blasting along the back roads in his Corvette with his wife telling him not to drive so fast, but the engine is so loud he usually can't hear her.

CPSIA information can be obtained
at www.ICGtesting.com
Printed in the USA
LVHW040917210421
685101LV00006B/692

9 781647 345631